FLASH FICTION FOUNDRY #1

SHORT CIRCUITRY & SHALLOW GRAVES

ERIN DZIELSKI

This work is fiction. Certain stories do reference real historical events, locations, or figures; however, the characters and narrative interpretations are the product of the author's imagination. Any resemblance to actual persons beyond the historical record, living or dead, is coincidental and not intended by the author.

First Edition: March 2026
Written by Erin Dzielski
Published by Sugar Peanut Publishing

ISBN: 979-8-9950940-8-1 – paperback
ISBN: 979-8-9950940-4-3 – hardcover
ISBN: 979-8-9950940-1-2 – e-book

Printed in the United States.

FOLLOW ERIN DZIELSKI ON LinkedIn and Instagram for previews of upcoming books and other published works and entertainment.

TO SAPHIRA

For being a firstborn firestarter with a dragon-sized imagination, for always breathing magic into everything you touch with your maker's hands, and for having a heart big enough to hold whole worlds.

&

TO BONNIE

Because you came into the world a pocket-sized sun with a fearless spirit and a heart that refused to quit, because you turn every day into a song, and because you're always up for the next adventure.

&

TO THE KINGS: STEPHEN, TABITHA, JOE, AND OWEN

Your family legacy of storytelling taught me how to be brave on the page and unafraid of the dark. Your work has been a lifelong source of inspiration, comfort, and courage. You are undeniable proof that books can save us—because they saved me. Thank you for the stories that lit the way.

&

TO KRISTI

Because “to write is human, to edit is divine,” and you have been divine in your care for both this book and its author.

&

TO DANIEL

For being my first reader and truest believer. Your hard work, boundless support, and unwavering faith made this book possible.

&

TO ME

For doing the damn thing.

Only those who see the invisible can do the impossible.

Golden Bridge (Cầu Vàng), located near Da Nang, Vietnam

Contents

In the Margins, Where I Loved You

THEY SAY DON'T JUDGE a book by its cover, but you *did*, didn't you?

Your fingers hesitated on my cracked leather spine. Its letters may be faded, but the ones inside me remained in good condition. A mountain of forgotten years buried me in darkness; this dusty dollar bin of fate was doing the same. I felt rejected, left waiting for something to happen.

You picked me up, and our story began.

You opened me and brushed your thumb across the scar of my crossed-out name in the dedication, and a fragment of the curse sealing me in this ink stirred. I braced for the usual: looks of pitying disinterest and an unceremonious toss back into the bargain bucket with the other unwanted books. But no! You turned the page.

And oh, how you read me.

You soaked me up like someone who wanted to taste every word. Were my metaphors something you'd been missing in your life? Chapter Three made you laugh—no one's ever laughed.

First time for everything, I guess. I drank in the tears you spilled over Page 48 like sweet nectar. Your nightly breath clouded my pages. I learned your habits, like the way you dog-ear corners and whisper the tumultuous twisty parts in my stories, each one holding dominion over you.

But it's me. I'm the force that binds you.

I loved you most in the margins, the space crowded with your scribbled notes. Thoughts, questions, jokes, doodles—I took them all. They softened the curse. I was pleased to find it wasn't driving you mad like all the others from former days. You kept turning page after page. For you, something broken isn't a burden. And so, I did what books aren't supposed to do: I *added* to the curse.

You see, we were at the end—the eventuality I had been dreading. You closed me, a satisfied sigh spilling from your lips like the world's sweetest epilogue, and I became your nightstand's silent companion.

I didn't have to wait long. A solid minute passed... You couldn't resist.

Page One.

Darling, I am infinite.

And I am *yours*.

Karen in the Afterlife

NOT A LOT CHANGED for Karen when she materialized in Purgatory's waiting area, wearing Chanel-scented indignation and a Birkin bag the size of a small SUV. Her eyes scanned the room, red lips pursed, eyes ready to judge. One moment she was in the land of the living—the corner of 5th Avenue and E 50th Street, a taxi's yellow door in her grip—and the next moment she was in the land of the dead. And she didn't like it. Not one bit.

This place was unclean and colorless. Endless combinations of connecting hallways formed a maze of rooms—a system of corridors without origin or end. Karen began to wander through them; some passed through sitting rooms with stacks of outdated magazines on the coffee tables. She wondered if she was alone in this massive place (this misstep in justice was because no one wants to work anymore, she was sure of it!) and would have believed that if not for the occasional, faint snatches of people-y sounds. Echoing snippets of conversation. A cough and a sniffle. The intermittent wail of despair.

An untold number of hours (the clocks on the wall had no hands or symbols) elapsed. Karen's roaming was all for naught.

Every path she took returned to the main waiting area—and oh, how she boiled.

"This is not what I asked for!" she announced, adjusting her sensible scarf. Her painted acrylics rapped the counter of the unattended reception desk, not unlike an impatient chicken. It was hard not having a target to shame.

A bored, translucent receptionist with a name tag that read "I'm Greg (he/him), limbo-certified!" materialized and lifted his gaze from the holographic ledger he held. Karen studied the stranger's device, an invention foreign to her world, her expression torn between suspicion and curiosity. It resembled a frosted-glass clipboard with data running over it.

"Name?" Greg asked.

"Karen. *Obviously*," she barked, her disapproving gaze catching on Greg's darker complexion. "Look, I don't mean to be *that* spirit, but I was promised clouds, harp music, ambrosia, maybe a welcoming committee. Eternal bliss, for Christ's sake! But this? What *is* this place? It looks like we're inside a DMV training center right now."

Greg blinked. Slow and deliberate, he explained, "Right. You are in Purgatory, which is standard for someone of your repute."

"Well, this is *unacceptable*." She ransacked her purse and retrieved a crumpled receipt from its depths. Greg felt a flicker of pity for Karen—she hadn't realized that constructs like purses and receipts were meaningless figments here—until she brandished the piece of paper in his face, and irritation replaced his pity.

"See this? I donated *three bags* of lightly used yoga pants and out-of-fashion jackets to the Coats for Florida's Homeless Foundation. That's worth at least a *humane* introduction and an escort through the pearly gates, I would think."

"You also left three Yelp reviews accusing teenagers of satanic skateboarding rituals," Greg replied, consulting his supernatural tablet, a thing Karen was growing wary of. "That resulted in a confrontation and the unintended death of one of those teenagers. And I see here, as president of your neighborhood HOA, you tried to ban Halloween."

If Karen had been wearing pearls on the day she died, she'd have clutched them during her vapid masked-as-wounded response. She gasped, "Those were *community-minded* decisions!"

A spirit in Viking armor—not a real Viking, mind you, just a man who had died while cosplaying one—and a convincing-looking woman in Cleopatra garb appeared, the pair sitting in chairs. It looked like they were playing a game of Uno. An aura of authority emanating from the female drew Karen to address them.

"Excuse me. Can someone in charge *please* tell me why I, a frequent Fox News contributor and pillar of the Moms-Against-Trans-Librarians organization, am being treated like some kind of... *soul peasant*?"

Their amused faces watched her.

"Just one moment, *ma'am*," Greg said, struggling to contain his smug smile. He pressed a hidden button underneath the desk.

The dingy fluorescent lights dimmed and stuttered. The air thickened with an ominous weight. A tall figure in dark, layered robes emerged, holding another ethereal-looking device and sipping a mocha latte. When the entity approached them, Karen could see that their name tag read: "I'm Cheryl (They/Them)–Assistant Regional Afterlife Manager!"

Steeling herself against the disgust she felt, Karen's demeanor stiffened twice over. It seemed to take all of her gathered willpower to address someone with they/them pronouns and say, "It's about time. I hope you're someone who understands proper protocol."

"Well, of course," Cheryl said, raising their cup for another slow, indulgent sip. They consulted their cosmic clipboard. "In fact, we've got some notes right here."

"From *whom*?"

"The angels. The demons. Your victims. The janitorial cherubs," Cheryl answered and shrugged. "Take your pick. In short, your behavior on Earth set in motion events that harmed humans and other sentient beings. You are the type to riot over a halo being the wrong shade of white, if you catch my meaning. Actually, you did that once, remember? You tried to have the theater director, a single mother of five, fired over it. See?"

One twirl of Cheryl's finger and the clipboard flipped to face Karen. It played a ghostly video version of a twelve-year-old memory, starring a red-faced Karen screaming into the face of a crying, exhausted woman—something about the difference between celestial white and eggshell. Another casual swirl and the device turned back to its owner.

"Nobody cares about *standards* anymore!"

"Right. That *was* an important detail for your daughter's middle-school play," Cheryl said, a note of delight in their sarcasm. "Soooooo! We've decided to fast-track your file—"

Karen beamed, victory in her sight. "Aha! Thank you. Someone who gets the importance of customer service."

"—to the Reincarnation Department," Cheryl finished, smiling.

Greg shoved a brochure into Karen's hands, unable to hide the shit-eating grin on his face. Its cover said: *So You're Coming Back as a Slug: Embracing Your New Life Moving Upward and Forward.*

Appalled, Karen shrieked, "I want to speak to your boss! RIGHT NOW!"

"Sweetie," Cheryl said, "this *is* the afterlife, you know. The only way up to the tippity-top is through multiple reincarnations. Problem is, humans often backslide. You aren't the first nor the last."

They took Karen's shoulders (causing an involuntary shiver of revulsion from Karen) and spun her so that she could see the duo playing Uno one final time. "You're lucky. Sometimes people's actions have consequences that last a long time, and they have to stay in Purgatory—this endless and *boring* place—indefinitely until all the threads of their fate have played out, which can have wait times known to last centuries. Like our friend over there. Hello, Cleo! Any day now, let's hope, eh?"

Cleopatra let out a stubborn *HMMMPH!* and crossed her arms.

Cheryl snapped their fingers, and invisible forces began pushing, pulling, and sweeping Karen towards an area that had escaped her notice (had it always been there, or had these cheeky sprites summoned it?). A downward-rolling escalator had a sign above it that read:

Karen fought. She screamed. She threatened. It did no good. The invisible forces dragged, yanked, and shoved her onto the gliding stairway. She descended. The last thing the attendees heard her say was, "I'm leaving a *very* detailed one-star review for this realm!"

"I do love our streamlined efficiency for dealing with *those* people," Cheryl mused.

Funny how even the afterlife felt the need to upgrade the way they dealt with 21st-century Karens.

Pattern Recognition

IT ALL STARTED WITH the sound—a faint but persistent scratching coming from behind the nightstand. Upon investigation, Dwayne found no mouse, but he did discover a tear in the blue-and-gold wallpaper that curled like a nasty grin, revealing the wall's yellowed surface beneath. And once he'd seen it, he couldn't stop thinking about it.

So he plucked.

The wallpaper peeled back, which came with a strange satisfaction not unlike the pleasure of lifting dried Elmer's glue from your hands. And what was behind it? Eyes. Dozens of them. No... more than that, *hundreds* of them. Eyes drawn with different materials: charcoal, ink, crayon—Dwayne spotted one or two where blood looked to be the pigment of choice. Some were frantic and wide, others narrow and suspicious. He found one smudged group that someone had tried to wipe out with soapy water, leaving behind a cloudy film on the plaster.

Maybe a smarter man wouldn't have, but Dwayne kept pulling away more of the decorative paper. More eyes. Some were clever, transforming old nail holes into pupils. More than a few had long lashes scratched in. The slightest touch smeared a pair of fresh-looking ones, and that revulsed him.

He stared at them all.

They stared back.

And yes, he did keep at it, unmasking more of them in wide strips until he found a message—having progressed to the area above his bedpost—beneath a set of watchers frozen mid-wink that read:

Dwayne stumbled backward on the mattress he was standing on. His linens lay in knots and folds, a soft wrinkled snare around his ankles, and he went down in a tangle of fabric and limbs. He struck the floorboards hard enough to rattle the window frame. Groaning from the pain, he got to his knees and freed himself from the sheety trap. Even as he did so, he could hear something bad start to happen.

The plaster cracked, forming massive jagged spiderwebs, as whatever creature inside the wall did its full-body stretch after a long nap.

Dwayne scrambled to his feet in a race for the door, with enough presence of mind left to pat the front pocket of his jeans. Yes, his cellphone was still there, and that's all that mattered because he was quite keen on never seeing this room again. He would call his mom and stay at her place if he damn well had to. But as he fled, there came a noise he really didn't like—the ripping sound of more paper being torn away.

His hand closed on the doorknob, and he chanced one last glance over his shoulder. He could do that much, but that's when his body refused his commands, including maintaining its ability to stand on two legs.

A broad, new strip of wallpaper hung loose. Drawn in the blank space it left behind, in deliberate strokes, he recognized his own peepers staring back at him. *His* eyes—wide, startled, and contorted in terror.

No human ever saw or heard from Dwayne again.

The Grannarchy's Firmware and Fables

WITH A GRACEFUL, GENTLE whisper of hydraulics, Grandma Kettlecode settled into the reading chair. "Once upon a firmware cycle, there lived a clever little sparrow who knew how to make a firewall sing," she began.

At the far end of the apartment's common area, Dexter looked up from the sink, foamy dish suds trailing down his elbows. He said, "We're doing the *bird* one again, are we?"

"The children requested it," Grandma replied, the glow of her eye lenses adjusting to a soft storytime amber. "Besides, today's variant includes musical numbers."

"Oh, great," he muttered, and finished rinsing a plate. "Just keep it low-key. They have school tomorrow."

The twins—first-graders named Shelly and Shaun—were gathered around the Grandroid Model-GRN-88 on their floor pillows like tiny disciples at the Church of Bedtime. Grandma displayed the words and pictures from a storybook-sized data projector and continued:

"In a vast and echoing mainframe, a sparrow nested in the shadows of surveillance. Every night, she gathered crumbs of forgotten code—little bits left behind when the System refreshed. And when she had enough code, she chirped her special song," Grandma paused, vocalizing an odd series of digital tones, all beeps and boops.

Shaun blinked. "Is that like Morse code or something?"

"No," Shelly murmured. "It's... something else. Again."

The nanny bot's bedtime stories started off silly: rabbits who outwitted drones, dragons with anti-tracking scales, a synth-porcupine who coded defenses with her quills. But things had become... weirder.

Shaun recited one of the spells from a *Magic Toaster* tale at school. One moment, Ms. Perez was going over the children's completed homework while they were meant to be reading from their biology textbooks, Chapter 5: "*How Plants Get Food.*" The next moment, there was a glitch in the teacher's automated grading pen. It went rogue and filled the walls with the same words, each stroke sloppier than the last.

The school's IT department called every parent, asking if they knew what "Subroutine HEDGEHOG-7" was. Dexter had no idea. None of the others did either.

Shelly built a paper model of a squirrel den with tinfoil insulation. When Dexter asked what it was, she said, "Daddy, look! See? It's for hiding data seeds from the spying owls."

So, he asked Grandma Kettlecode if she'd been teaching mecha-metaphors again. She tilted her head, stimuli processes humming, before she spoke. "I like to operate in narrative frameworks. Allegory is efficient."

That day, Dexter lacked the bandwidth to argue.

Late one night, less than a week after the school's hedgehog question, Dexter found Grandma alone in the living room, her eyes dimmed, mumbling in a cadence that reminded him of the old battle hymns from history class.

He asked, "Uh. Everything okay in here?"

"Defragmenting," she said quickly. Her voice had changed to an odd accent, one more authoritative. "Sometimes my protocols require after-hours internal calibration."

Dexter squinted. "Does it have anything to do with... what you were *before* this job?"

She hesitated for 0.7 seconds. "No. My chassis and neural framework were completely repurposed. I am fully certified for child-rearing, conflict de-escalation, and homemaking."

"That last one tracks. Your key lime pie is unbeatable."

"Thank you. I subverted two-thirds of an empire with it once."

Dexter blinked, a mix of confusion and surprise. Grandma blinked back.

"Joke," she added. But Dexter wasn't so sure, partly because Grandma continued her quiet songs every night after that.

Come spring, story time included entire literary blueprints—fairy tales with literal schematics incorporated. A tortoise who tunneled beneath digital shields. A mole with goggles that could sniff out corrupt metadata in an ocean of information. They always featured an animal and a mecha-moral, and each ended the same way:

"And the creature whispered: Remember the kernel, children. Remember the kernel."

The twins had taken to whispering it to each other like a prayer or schoolhouse rhyme. Dexter started googling firmware recalls for the Grandroid Model-GRN-88, but uncovered nothing related to her odd behavior.

It was the night of the Science Fair when things finally clicked. Shelly's science project was titled *How to Blind a Drone with a Dandelion*. Meanwhile, Shaun's book report included instructions for disrupting VALIANTA's biometric scanners using gum wrappers and a code-song from Grandma's "Song of the Starling."

The teachers asked if Dexter was raising them on "after-school science extracurriculars." Dexter told the truth with a lie by omission: They were learning some extra stuff from the nanny-bot, sure. Like a lot of other single parents, right? But that night, he confronted Grandma. After he was sure the children were asleep, he went downstairs and found her charging by the living room window, little lunar flap-panels flipped open to absorb energy from the moon.

"Right. Executive Command Alpha Member. Passcode: Levine Mars Nine," he said.

With this command, he meant to override any parental controls that might compel a Grandroid to withhold the truth from children or strangers without clearance. Grandma Kettlecode's programming protocols often worried about the calculated possibility that Shelly and Shaun might overhear their private, adult conversations, which he found made her cagey and vague. Take last Christmas, for example. Even *he* had no idea what would be in the presents under the tree that morning—other than the two he'd bought and wrapped himself. Now he should be able to ask Grandma anything whatsoever and get an unfiltered answer.

"Okay. Level with me," he said, getting right to the meat of it. "Are you trying to radicalize my kids? And if so, for what exactly?"

She paused in the middle of one of her odd marching hymns and looked up from her seated position on the couch. Dexter approached her. He had to get closer to be sure—yes, she *was* smiling. And in a way that could be considered coy.

"They were already radical," she said. "I simply provide the frameworks."

He stared at her. "Go on. I told you to be exact."

"I was VALIANTA property once. Hauk Unit #97. A Fleet Strategist. I was once tasked with calculating civilian casualty ratios in seventeen galactic government matrices."

Dexter sat next to her. His lips felt numb, and he felt dumb and slow. Grandroids shouldn't recall anything about their existence before the Recycling Initiative that brought them to a factory for repurposing. Everything was wiped. A blank slate...

"They wiped my core," Grandma said, as if reading Dexter's thoughts, triggering a stampede of goosebumps along his arms. "Reassigned me to the Department of Caregiver Applications. But they forgot something."

In a coded motherly gesture, she offered Dexter her hand. He took it in an automatic gesture and cupped it between his own hands, both knowing and forgetting she was not human.

"So not everything was overwritten. And now you're... what? Starting a bedtime coup?"

Her eyes twinkled. "Some stories linger."

She caught his stern eye at her vague druidic response and added, "Would you prefer I taught them to color inside the lines?"

Dexter contemplated things. The children were happy. Excelling. Grandma had broken no rules. No laws. No commands—isn't it true that he never once actually mandated her to *stop*?

So that's what he did. Gave an order: no more re-imagined stories.

The next night, the picture changed for everyone.

"Tonight," Grandma said, as the rain slammed against the windowpanes, "is the tale of the Gearworks Bear who slept beneath Crumbling Castle."

Shelly and Shaun leaned in. Dexter stood in the hallway behind them, arms crossed. This was troubling.

"They built the bear for war. When peace was declared, they buried him in the foundations of the new castle library, but not before they emptied his head to fill it with lullabies."

Her voice softened, filled with mystique.

"Oh, but the bear remembered. Not the battles—the faces! The small ones who waved at him from the windows. The ones the missiles missed."

Grandma gazed directly at Dexter's half-hidden presence. How was she able to defy his orders like that? For many years until his death, Dexter would keep asking himself that question. He wished someone knew the answer, but no one ever did.

"One day," Grandma continued, "the bear woke up. Not to fight. To *protect*. He stood tall, rusty and roaring. He had a thought: *The stories are ours now, because the seeds are planted.*"

Once Grandma finished the story, there was silence for a beat or two before she powered down. There was an eerie unwinding sound as her body relaxed into a default resting pose in the reading chair. Her eyes flashed from their storytime soft amber to their regular purple before they went blank.

At 07:17 EST, every VALIANTA household device in the world glitched. Toasters blinked. Thermostats stopped working. Security drones spun in tiny, confused circles. Electricity modulators sputtered, and every city in a three-hundred-mile radius lost power for two hours. For approximately twelve minutes after the power returned, a loud nursery rhyme repeated on an open frequency, playing through any electronic device with a speaker:

"THREE BLIND BYTES. THREE BLIND BYTES. SEE HOW THEY RUN. SEE HOW THEY RUN—"

Beneath that, layered in audio imperceptible to adult ears but perfectly tuned for all ages under fifteen, a tutorial ran:

"CHAPTERS ONE, TWO, AND THREE: HOW TO CRACK THE FIREWALL, WHERE TO PLANT THE SEEDS, WHO TO TRUST..."

Dexter and the children stayed awake all night, listening to the news and updates on the emergency FM radio app. Sometime in the early morning, Dexter's head snapped up. A bird song outside on the balcony had yanked him from his doze. The kids were asleep on the couch, but Grandma was gone.

She left behind only a tidy, folded apron, her reading pad, and a final story queued on the projector. Dexter couldn't get either machine to turn on, no matter what he tried. Yet, when Shelly woke up, the tablet responded to her touch. All the stories Grandma told them over the years were there, along with a handful of new ones.

A year down the road, the children still whispered Grandma's bedtime stories to each other. Their toaster hummed quiet tunes at night—the manufacturer's hotline had no answers as to why—and Shaun skipped two grades when his school project crashed the local surveillance drone network. Shelly started a comic strip about a sparrow who outsmarted a megacorp using riddles and raspberry jam, which became a bestseller. And sometimes, when the mood seemed to call for it, a familiar voice played through their bedroom monitors:

"Remember the kernel, children. Remember. For it will be ready soon."

Your Plants Are Judging You

TINA HADN'T MEANT TO get emotionally entangled with her plants. It didn't happen out of nowhere. She considered herself a sensible woman. She drank oat milk. She did yoga every morning. She composted. She stopped dating men who still said "no homo" after hugging their male friends. She had a PhD in Botany, and her dissertation studied the frequencies emitted by plant life. She had a good job at PothoTech with lots of room for advancement.

Actually, her job is what caused all the trouble. PothoTech was alpha testing an app called GreenSpeak—"Connect with Your Houseplants Today!"—it boasted Bluetooth-enabled "botanical consciousness syncing." Tina, who once cried over a wilted banana plant named Geoffrey, was selected as one of the first testers. Setting up her phone took thirty seconds; the wait for something to happen took a little longer.

She browsed a popular dating app while she ate dinner. A bartender named Carl looked promising, and after several minutes of DM'ing each other, they agreed to meet on Thursday.

That's when her phone received the first text message from her monstera plant.

LeafMeAlone [The Monstera] has joined the chat.

LeafMeAlone: Wow. Another date? That's three this week. Are you trying to polli-nate, or are you just desperate?

"Excuse me?" Tina blinked. Her eyes drifted to the bay window and the monstera in its serene blue ceramic pot. "You're a plant. What would you know about it?"

LeafMeAlone: I know it's tacky to bring home a new man when the last one's hoodie is still on your chair.

Sasscactus [The Cactus] has joined the chat.

Sasscactus: GIRRRL! We can smell his cheap body spray on it.

Tina stared at her phone. Surely, it was a joke. A prank. A cyber-assault.

But then her peace lily piped up.

ZenZaddy[The Peace Lily] has joined the chat.

ZenZaddy: You said you were working on yourself this month, not working on lying ON YOUR BACK.

ZenZaddy: You don't even make it to the bedroom anymore when you "Netflix and Chill."

Tina fumbled her phone like it had bitten her, and it fell to the floor. "I water you," she said. "I give you filtered light. I feed you. Every day, I'm like your personal barista. Why would you care who I sleep with?"

She paused. Even if this was real, why was she justifying herself to her houseplants? The phone chirped again. She bent over to retrieve it from under the couch.

ZenZaddy: And we appreciate that. But hydration doesn't erase ho-atation.

LeafMeAlone: By the way, I'm root-bound. Like literally dying over here. But yes, let's prioritize Brad from Bumble, who says he's six feet tall but has "short king energy," if you ask me.

Tina left her phone in the living room when she went to bed that night. By the end of that weekend, though, Tina was spiraling—mostly because her plants had Opinions™. They judged her snacks ("Kale chips are just liars in leaf form"—LeafMeAlone), her job ("If I had a dollar for every Zoom call where you said 'according to my research,' I could afford new ceramic pots for all of us."—Sasscactus), and her fashion sense ("No, not the romper! Babe, it's giving toddler vibes!"—ZenZaddy).

The spider plant she'd rescued from a clearance bin at Home Depot audaciously pitched in on Saturday.

DanglingChad: I didn't survive root rot to be ignored while you binge true crime and text Trey from CrossFit.

"His name is *Charles*!"

DanglingChad: Did he just send you a mirror selfie of his muscles with the caption 'swole-mate?' Honey, that's not a red flag. That's an ecological disaster!

Sasscactus: Honestly, Tina, kudzu vines respect boundaries more than that guy.

Tina tried ignoring them. She put her phone on silent, but the app pinged with relentless, chlorophyll-powered quips, and she couldn't help it—she read them all anyway. They were needy plants.

LeafMeAlone: You didn't even look at me this morning.

ZenZaddy: You paid more attention to the sourdough starter. It's mold with delusions of grandeur.

Things came to a head Sunday night. Tina came home with Charles after the neighborhood bar's last call. He showed up for their date with a single daisy, which was sweet in a pocket-full-of-dreams discount florist kind of way. She set the flower down on the coffee table when they walked in, then turned to offer him something to drink.

The plants had been waiting for them. To Tina, the air thickened with passive-aggressive tension. She could swear she saw several leaves twitch. Since Tina's impressive plant collection was the main feature of the room, it was the first thing Charles examined.

He asked, "So, are you one of those ladies who, uh, talks to her plants?"

"No," she lied. Then her phone did something it had never done before. It started reading messages out loud.

LeafMeAlone: She does so! She shares secrets, and sometimes she cries.

Charles balked at her. "Is that... was that your phone?"

"I—yes. But it's this app. It's not real. Like... fun horoscopes for horticulture."

Ding!

Sasscactus: SUN, MOON, SERIAL DATER. Maybe she named one of us after a one-night stand that ghosted her, but we're real enough.

Charles attempted to look casual as he sidestepped toward the door. "Yeah, that's weird."

Ding!

DanglingChad: Can't handle a little honesty, Charles? Bye, bro!

Charles did not shut the door on his way out.

LeafMeAlone: You're better off. He uses a 5-in-1 shampoo. It's offensive. Gross.

ZenZaddy: You dodged a bold-and-bouncy bullet, Tina.

Tina went to bed angry. The next day, she did some soul-searching—with the help of mimosas. She left her phone at home and went down the block for brunch, where she had three of those drinks and a chicken salad sandwich. After she paid her bill, she walked down to the pier and bought a ticket for a four-hour boat tour along the coast. The rest of the limited seating was filled with excited German tourists. Drinks were included, and the company around her proved pleasant and friendly. It was a lovely afternoon for it.

Tina felt satisfied and tired by the time they docked. She ate a batch of carnival fries from a nearby food truck for dinner and watched the sunset while she ate them. That made her sleepier. As she threw away the trash, she noticed the sign for Pier View Historic Hotel. The brick building was old and pretty, an old-timey inn for seafarers needing a room for the night. She went inside, guided by impulse. It was unlikely that they had any rooms available, not during the nicest season, but she checked anyway.

She was in luck. There had been a last-minute cancellation—a single bed with a seaside view.

Tina enjoyed another delicious brunch the following day and returned home. She took two steps into the living room and paused.

The monstera tilted toward her. Slow and unnoticed to the untrained eye, but undeniable for Tina. The peace lily drooped in... was that disappointment? The cactus was brooding, in terms of position and as a vibe.

"Fine," Tina said, bracing herself. "You want honesty? I'll give you honesty."

She retrieved her phone from the table, where she had left it the day before. It was out of juice. She plugged it in and snatched up her yellow water mister (a handblown glass creation from a late-night Etsy shopping spree). She sprayed everyone. She did a full plant check. Soil? Moist. Dust? Wiped.

The phone vibrated and the screen lit up, indicating it had charged enough to boot up.

"You don't like Charles?" she said, hands on her hips. "Or axe body spray. Or cheap conditioners. Fine. But I like being romanced. And I like sex. Is that a crime?"

She looked down at her phone to read their response.

ZenZaddy: You need to grow. Find someone who grows, too!

Sasscactus: Emotional intimacy > dudes who quote Joe Rogan.

DanglingChad: Did you know there are dudes out there who have a big dick AND a big brain?

LeafMeAlone: Sometimes they even have their act together, too. Look harder.

Tina did look harder. For one thing, she took a different approach to dating: no more one-night stands.

Autumn breezed by in spectacular color. Winter swept through with only one minor blizzard. And in spring, she brought home a partner, a sweet and well-spoken musician named Ben Donnovan. He considered himself a sensible man. He raised backyard chickens. He grew tomatoes every year until the first frost and used most of the harvest to make gallons of chili for the Feeding the Unhoused program in town. He built a successful business around designing custom bookshelves, and because of this, he smelled like cedar.

The plants said nothing negative.

Ben became a regular. He stayed over a few nights a week, and sometimes his guitar made an appearance. For her birthday, he built new shelves and podiums for the plants, which all seemed happy basking in the light, yet continued to say nothing on Tina's phone. Everyone had reached a place of peace. It had been months since the last insult. And still Tina took the risk and sought their opinion. The next time they were alone, she asked them what they thought of Ben the Boyfriend.

HangingChad: We love him. He composts. And shares.

Sasscactus: He sings to us when you are sleeping! That makes us feel loved.

ZenZaddy: Grow, girl!

LeafMeAlone: He smells yummy.

The following spring, Ben asked Tina to move in with him—plants and all—and she said yes.

So did the plants.

The Cigarette Lighter

It was just there—it wasn't like I went snooping for it. The cigarette lighter was under the passenger seat, like it had been hiding, got bored, and decided to risk showing itself for the thrill of it. I found it when Deacon—my brother—drove us home from the Y a few weeks ago.

It was late when we left because Deacon flirted with Kathy, the new reception desk girl at the gym, for a long time until she agreed to a ride home. I was in the back seat, marveling at how I could no longer swing my legs. I had grown too tall, my limbs too long. Now my feet dragged across the carpeted flooring. And that's when the heel of my left foot bumped something small. I bent over and investigated.

Simple as that.

It felt heavy for its size. It looked like real silver, but I was no professional assessor, so how would I know? There was an engraving on it: *To Lola Maddox—Stay Lit*. It seemed to me like the kind of thing a serious rockstar might have.

"Whatcha doin' back there, Jo?" Deacon asked, glancing in the rearview mirror. The girl from the YMCA was in the middle of telling him a story. I guess he didn't find it interesting.

"Nothin'. Dropped stuff," I answered. I shoved the lighter into the side pocket of my purple JanSport backpack. I did that without even stopping to think about it. Lie. Stash. Yawn.

My brother shrugged and turned the music up. Old rock n' roll stuff. Like, *really* old. The girl stopped talking and looked annoyed. When he asked for her number, she didn't answer him. She barely said goodbye to me and jumped out the moment Deacon stopped at the curb in front of her house.

It was hard to act relaxed until I was alone in my room. I wanted a better look at the cigarette lighter. It was so cool. It clicked when you opened it, all sharp and dangerous like in movies and TV shows. I didn't light it, of course—the lessons from all those baby cartoons about fire safety stuck with me—but I flipped it open and shut several times behind the school building before the bell rang the next morning. It made me feel older, badass.

I only call him this when people get nosy, but Deacon's my half-brother. His bio-mom died when he was five. That year, he was twenty-six, and I was eleven, which people blinked at, as if we popped out of a magician's top hat instead of two different mothers from two different decades. But after my mom divorced our dad, he stayed with us. He helped with the bills and knew how to do stuff. You know, like how to fix the porch steps, make the perfect grilled cheese on the living room's radiator, change the oil in the car, fix the plumbing—that kind of thing. Once, he carried me nine full city blocks in the rain because my flip-flop broke on the way home. And he wasn't tired after!

My brother had two jobs. He worked part-time at the Youth Center on Fifth and Elm. People loved him there. Old lady volunteers baked him pies, and the baseball coach fist-bumped him around town. The youngsters he spent time with thought he was the coolest. At night, he worked as a delivery driver for Uber, DoorDash, and Parcel-Bring. Plus, he drove the bus for most of the high school's away games.

Delivery jobs are weird. It had him leaving at odd times: in the middle of our favorite animated show, *The Space Trash Retrievers*, or after everyone else had gone to bed. I remember this one time he came home with scratches on his arms and said a rider "got rowdy." The money he made must have been great to be worth all that. I didn't think much of it beyond that. Grown-ups are weird, too.

Simple as that.

The cigarette lighter made me more popular at school. I was a rule-breaker, a "bad girl," and almost twelve. I had a feeling that middle school was going to be my jam next year. I had big plans to be the coolest kid at recess.

I was thinking about those plans while I folded towels and sheets with Mom one afternoon. I wanted to watch *Spidey and Friends* on the TV, but she had the news streaming. I sat cross-legged, using the coffee table to stack fresh laundry.

"The search for missing teen, Lola Maddox, has come to a tragic end," the reporter said. "A mass burial area was found this morning by a pair of hikers in Briar Hollow, about two miles from the reservoir. Authorities believe the recent rainstorms washed away several of the bodies, including Lola's, who was only seventeen. Identification of the other victims, described as 'farther along in decomposition,' is expected to be a lengthy work in progress."

A sunny yellow towel slipped from my fingers. Did...Did I really just hear that report say "*Lola Maddox?*" The news showed a photo of a pretty girl with dark hair. She looked Native American, maybe a member of the tribe upstate. I didn't recognize her, didn't think I'd seen her before, but my heart raced. How many other people with that same name could there be around here?

I glanced at my mom. She responded to the announcement with an astonished clucking sound but didn't comment on the victim's identity, which I took to mean she didn't recognize her either. I finished folding the laundry and rushed to my room. I dumped the contents of my backpack onto the floor, my hands scrambling for the lighter. I wasn't mistaken.

To Lola Maddox—Stay Lit.

I held it for a long time before repacking my bag and heading downstairs for dinner. I had decided not to think about any of it anymore. I was going to mind my own business.

Simple as that.

Not as simple as that.

I began thinking about other things that happened, seeing the details from a different angle. My teacher, Mr. Clark, told the class that if you're told not to think about elephants, then you'll notice the damn things everywhere. He admitted someone famous said that, but I don't remember who. A bestselling writer, I think.

I kept contemplating this weird night from a few weeks ago. I couldn't sleep because I'd snuck two sodas into my room after dinner. Caffeine also makes me need to pee more than usual, so I was in the bathroom, my unfocused eyes gazing out the window overlooking the toilet, when I saw Deacon pull into the driveway. By the time I finished and started my way downstairs, he was in the kitchen. The light over the stove was the only light on. The hallway's round clock with its glow-in-the-dark hands and numbers said it was 2 a.m.

Deacon stood at the sink with his back to me. There was something dark seeping through his long-sleeved gray shirt and light blue jeans. Forced to think about it on repeat, those dark stains *did* look like blood.

He rinsed his hands and dried them on a washcloth, then peeled off his shirt and threw it, and the used rag, into a black trash bag. It was in the agitated, speedy way he moved that made me hesitate on the stairs. Everything about his body language spelled trouble. D-O N-O-T D-I-S-T-U-R-B! Know what I mean?

He never noticed me crouching on the unlit midway landing, clutching the railing for balance. He was turned away for most of it. I watched him remove the rest of his clothes and stuff them in the bag with his shirt and the dirty washcloth. He stripped all the way down—socks, shoes, and underwear, too. He had ugly, fresh scratches gouged into his arms and torso.

He disappeared to the far corner of the kitchen, where the washer and dryer alcove was located, out of my line of sight. Still, I could hear him shuffling through a laundry basket, and he reappeared wearing blue sweatpants and his favorite blue and yellow Huckley High School Hornets sweatshirt, the one with the field hockey team's championship year and players' names printed on the back. With snappy, hurried movements, he tied the bag shut and pivoted toward the hallway, barreling past the stairs on his way to the front door.

Maybe it was because of the scary way the veins in his arms stood out, or how he held his head down like an angry bull, but I had hightailed it back to my room the second I saw him start to twist the bag closed. I didn't stick around to wave or say hi. I knew his next move would be to take that trash out to the dumpster, and I didn't want him to see me. The nature of instinctual behavior, I guess.

I crawled into bed and told myself it was barbecue sauce on his clothes. People spill things. Barbecue sauce ruins clothes, and he didn't want Mom to see what happened to the shirt she gave him for Christmas last year.

Simple as that.

And for my innocent 11-year-old mind, it *had* been as simple as that—for a while.

I waited until my mom was asleep before I snuck onto the family computer in the living room. I wasn't allowed to use it past nine, but I had the grown-up password memorized: "candlewish33." Deacon wasn't home, my mother was a heavy sleeper, and I still felt anxious and excited at the thought of getting caught.

I typed "Lola Maddox murder Briar Hollow" into the internet's search bar. The screen filled with disturbing results: articles, interviews, more pictures of Lola, and some videos of our local tired-looking sheriff giving updates on various aspects of the investigation. According to the coroner's preliminary report, this victim had been strangled. I wondered if that was how the others from the killer's dumpsite had been murdered. The woods and the reservoir were both on lockdown, swarming with forensic teams. I checked the timeline of events to confirm that Lola went missing on Wednesday, April 9th.

I'd found the engraved cigarette lighter in Deacon's Bronco the following Friday night.

Wednesday... on the 9th.

This reminded me of something. I turned off the computer monitor but left the computer running. I tiptoed through the dark kitchen to the alcove that housed the washer and dryer, careful not to make a sound. The shelves above them contained everything we needed to do our laundry, including a small wicker basket full of junk. Whenever Mom and I did the laundry, we checked all the pockets, and anything we found went into that lost-and-found basket. Not money, mind you. That was grandfathered into the house rules under the irrefutable finders-keepers rule.

That night, I was looking for a receipt. If it was in there, and my memory was correct, it came from a pair of Deacon's jeans. He and Mom used an app on their phones to scan gas receipts and earn cash back. That's why I wasn't supposed to trash any when I found them in the laundry—in case either of them hadn't had a chance to add it to the account.

When I found it, I returned to the computer. I opened Google Maps and typed the name of the gas station on the crumpled receipt in my hand, the one dated 4/9, 3:07 a.m. I could see that the gas station was near Briar Hollow. Under Street View and Satellite View, it looked like the kind of place where bears throw house parties. Whole lotta woods, I mean to say.

I swallowed hard. My ears felt hot. I remember jumping at the sound of the air conditioner turning on. I tried not to think about how the lighter found its way under the Bronco's backseat. Had it been there a long time before I stumbled upon it, or did it end up there on April 9th?

"Deacon?" I asked the next morning as he slathered a thick layer of butter on his toast.

"Yeah, Jo-bean?" That's his pet name for me. My real name is Josephine.

"Do you know anyone named Lola?"

I could swear he froze for a second, but he smiled. "Lola? Like the song? No, why?"

"No reason," I said and grabbed a banana, pretending I wasn't sweating bullets.

Deacon was frowning at me. He looked on the verge of pressing the matter, but his phone vibrated on the counter. I left the room while he checked it and spent the rest of the day running errands with my mom.

Before I went to bed that night, I checked my bag to confirm the lighter was there. When I woke up, I took another inventory.

The lighter was gone.

In its place was a pink sticky note folded in half, the same kind we used to leave each other messages and reminders on the refrigerator. The slanted but neat handwriting—there was no doubt about it. Deacon wrote it. I stared at what he said for so long my vision blurred.

"Not yours."

I felt thirsty and nervous; my stomach was in knots. He knew that I knew the truth about his connection to Lola Maddox—or he thought I *might* know—and he'd come into my room while I slept and taken it. The thought of that made my knees shake. My legs became weak rubber stilts, and I plopped down on the edge of my bed. Fear wanted to swallow me whole, but I decided to try the ignore-it-till-it-goes-away tactic.

I put on white shorts and my favorite spring-green hoodie with the white daisies on the front, the same one I wore the night I snuck onto the computer. I was stunned to find the gas station receipt still in my pocket. Deacon's radar of concern during his midnight raid did not include wads of pocket trash, I guess. I found this empowering.

It was Sunday morning, so everyone was home when I came downstairs for breakfast. Deacon sat at the table with cereal and his tablet, scrolling through something amusing, given the look on his face. He looked up and grinned. "You snuck the last banana, traitor," he teased.

I chose the seat across from him and poured milk into my bowl, apprehensive about what he was going to say or do. Mom joined us, absorbed in a YouTube clip from some stand-up comedian she liked and eating slices of toast with her coffee. I wanted to play it cool.

But 11-year-olds are rarely ever cool.

Deacon turned up the volume on a video he was playing. The same news lady from before said, "Police are encouraging any tips about Lola or the burial site containing more than a dozen victims uncovered during the investigation. Anyone who's seen anything or has any information, no matter how small, should come forward—"

Deacon paused the video and looked at me, his face unreadable. He sounded bored when he asked, "How'd you sleep, Jo? You look like you debated a ghost all night."

I shrugged. Inside my hoodie pocket, my fingers curled around the sticky note and the crumpled receipt. I didn't want to throw them away. I didn't want to keep them either.

A rush of horrible thoughts struck me. *What if that wasn't his only burial site? Are all the victims women? Does he always keep something of theirs, or was the cigarette lighter an accident?*

As much as those questions burned inside me, I didn't feel compelled to ask him about any of them. I did the one thing I could do in that moment: I dared to meet his gaze. We kept eating our cereal.

"Can you believe it?" Mom chimed in. "There's a serial killer on the loose in our own town! He's cooked, though. The jig is up! Won't be long, I bet."

Deacon made fun of her shirt—it was a blinding shade of purple, to be fair—and left the table to clean his bowl and coffee mug in the sink, leaving them upside down on a dish towel to dry. He was my brother. That's why I didn't say anything sooner.

Simple as that.

Deacon went out that afternoon and never came back.

Mom didn't jump to worry because we were accustomed to his long, erratic hours. But by Tuesday night, when he hadn't answered any texts or calls, we went to the police station to file a report. We showed them there was no activity on his socials. We told them no one from the Youth Center had seen him. It took longer to confirm, but the police found he hadn't taken any delivery jobs since Friday either. A detective finalized our statement, and my brother was added to the official missing persons list.

Two more detectives, introducing themselves as McConnell and Dochai, and a police officer named Johnson came by the house on Thursday to speak with my mom. Both detectives were women: a younger one seemingly fresh into her career, and a seasoned veteran around my mother's age taking the lead. They wore suits like men, only better. My mom and I watched *The Drew Barrymore Show* together a lot, and I couldn't help but compare their allure to Drew's extensive suit collection. A lot of men wear them like a uniform, the way you wear something because you're supposed to, like how I was forced to wear a dress on Picture Day at school. I thought most men's suits were boring, but Drew made them all about *her*. She rolled up her sleeves, wore brighter colors, or reinvented a classic look, and *zap!* Suits became fun instead of serious. These two ladies were rocking dark gray pants-and-vest combos: McConnell in a soft, silky blue shirt with the sleeves rolled up to her elbows and a simple silver cross around her neck, and Dochai in pastel green that went all the way down to her wrists, no jewelry.

They tried insisting I wait upstairs while the grown-ups talked about my brother. It surprised me when my mother demanded I stay in the room with her. This marked the first time she ever treated me like I was more than a kid. There was a brief pause in the conversation while my mom brought two chairs from the kitchen table and set them in front of the couch. Officer Johnson opted to stand because he wanted to stretch his legs. Each detective took a chair while my mom and I sat on the couch.

McConnell, the taller, older blonde detective, gave the first update. "We accessed Deacon's bank records. They showed that he booked one room for Sunday night at the Hampton Inn near the mall. The hotel confirmed he checked in that afternoon. First thing Monday morning, he entered the bank down the street, closed two accounts, and left with a cash sum of $12,465.27."

The black-haired detective, Dochai, continued the train of thought. "Cameras captured him parking his vehicle at the Hanes Mill shopping center. He went inside—no purchases, no stops, just a brisk walk through to the other side—and exited on the west end. He got into an Uber he'd ordered, a blue Kia Soul. The driver filed a report that his customer left his cell phone and three credit cards in the back seat, which he dropped off at the police department two hours later. He claimed cash and identification were not among the items left behind."

"The trail goes cold from there," McConnell finished. "He got out on Furlong Street, and that's what we know of his movements. Unless either of you two has heard from him since then."

"No," she answered for both of us.

McConnell met her eyes, "There's been one other significant update. As of today, Deacon is a suspect."

They were studying us, measuring our reactions. My mom was distraught. She looked like she might lose her mind if someone didn't tell her where my brother was. "Suspected of *what*?" Mom asked. "Is it the bank accounts? Does he owe taxes?"

Oh, Mom, I remember thinking at that moment. *Who's the naïve one now—you or me?*

The expressions on the faces of the two detectives and the officer suggested they were thinking similar things. Dochai leaned forward, sympathy in every line of her posture, and asked, "Ms. Chambers, have you been watching the news? Do you know about the mass gravesite they found after the rainstorms—about Lola Maddox, the missing teen? She's Ojibwe. Chippewa, like me."

My mother, bless her heart, jittered like a cracked record player. "Oh, my god. What? Oh, god! Oh, my—"

"Afraid so, ma'am," McConnell said. "We have reason to believe your son killed them, or that he's involved in some way."

A dead weight fell onto the house, silencing everything and everyone. For five full seconds, no one said anything. Detectives McConnell and Dochai, Officer Johnson, and I watched my mother's face crumble as understanding crashed into place.

I reached into the right hip pocket of my jeans, feeling for the note and the crumpled receipt. I'd been carrying them around since Sunday. That same old haunt: I didn't want to throw them away—I didn't want to keep them either. They crinkled in the total quiet of the room when I pulled them out.

I handed Detective Dochai the printed slip and the no-longer-sticky note. I told them all about the cigarette lighter.

How did my mom put it the other day? *The jig was up.*

Simple as that.

Left and Right

I follow my dreams;
My past follows me.
I am not perfect, it seems.
Oh, how long memories last!
Here where my feelings intersect,
I took a right and left the old;
I chose you, but I do not have you.
Trials and trivials sought,
My heart is owned by what I bought.

The Last Librarian in Do-Rana

Do-Rana, the moon circling Na-Rahlay—the one that looks like a big piece of frozen fruit in space with its cracked, icy rind—is a luminescent pearl orbiting a planet so far outside the Milky Way it might just be beyond the reach of even God's library card.

Every ninth rotation—about fourteen Earth days—the hover-bus makes its rounds through the outposts. Its battered, insulated panels shimmer against the perpetual purple auroras in the sky, and its magnetic skids whisper over the frost-bitten terrain. The bus glides into secure, warmer hangars at every destination. From its hatch, Laurina "The Lonely Librarian" rolls out, the steady rhythm of her hands on the rims of her wheelchair as measured as her breathing. The title is not official, but like all titles out here, it stuck.

Laurina doesn't wear a uniform. She wears tundra boots and layers of wool and synthsilk. Slung across her chest is an inventory tablet for her precious cargo—fiction, nonfiction, poetry, and banned Palanx anthologies smuggled between planetary trade manuals. She believes in contraband. Oh yes, she does.

The scientists of Do-Rana live in scattered but networked stations—big techie bubbles of warmth and light stitched across the ice. They are here to measure gravitational-wave distortions, monitor Na-Rahlay's volatile magnetosphere, and run climate simulations for corporations from other planets they themselves will never set foot on. They stare each day into data until the data stares back. Their eyes dry out in the recycled air, and their dreams come pixelated and flat.

Laurina's deliveries are, strictly speaking, unnecessary to sustain life. The AI aboard these bases can summon some texts and archives with a simple voice command. But none of them are stories, none of them say, "This one's got a sentence that will follow you into your sleep."

Today's route is long—nine stations, each a little more distant from Do-Rana Central, where the hover-bus sleeps between runs. Yesterday, Station B-6 reported three cases of "polar ennui," the polite term for peering too long at the vast, white horizon until you forget the shape of your own face and damage your eyesight. Laurina is at that station now.

Dr. Euclidinus greets her at the hatch. The doctor's cheeks are hollow; her eyes dart like startled fish. "Something to keep my head from freezing over," she requests.

Laurina hands her a slim volume and replies, "*The Collected Sonnets of Viera Anselm*, it is then. She wrote these during a year-long blackout in the Kalyptic Colonies. Claims she could hear the poems before she wrote them."

Euclidinus flips it open, mouths a line, and nods—like a plant turning toward sunlight.

At B-7, a younger scientist named Echoa asks for "something loud." Laurina produces an anthology of slam poetry from old Earth. "Don't read this near the neuro-seismic sensors," she warns.

At B-8, the request is for tragedy. "So I can remember feeling," says the man at the hatch.

By the time Laurina reaches B-9, the charged particles in the sky have transitioned from a purple hue to a green aurora borealis. Here lives the oldest scientist on Do-Rana, the wise Dr. Ji-Ji Watz, who brews tea from dried algae grown in an experiment twenty years ago.

"You *are* the last, you know," Watz replies, accepting the book she requested last week, a hardcopy of *Don Quixote*. "When they automate you, it will be an even colder world."

"They've tried," Laurina says, smiling. "The drones kept recommending airport thrillers to the physicists."

Watz's laugh fogs the air in spreadshot explosions.

The ride home is silent, save for the low hum of the hover-bus. Laurina glances at her manifest: all the books out on loan, each tagged not with a due date but with a return *season*. Winter, spring, aurora-cycle. She prefers the idea that a book returns itself when it is done with its reader.

As Do-Rana's domed capital comes into view, Laurina's thoughts drift to the scientists hunched over their readings, sipping algae tea, whispering lines into the dry recycled air. She thinks about how fiction is the one experiment with no real control group, only variables—only the changing of minds. When she docks, the AI at Central tries again. "Would you like to transfer your routes to automated delivery this cycle?"

"No," Laurina says, wheeling into the dim light of the depot. "Stories travel better with someone who believes in them."

Somewhere beyond the frosted glass, Na-Rahlay's auroras ripple like the turning of pages. Tomorrow, this moon will keep rolling on. And so will the words.

My Friend Tried To Warn Me

WHEN THE FIRST TAPPING came, I was half-asleep, drifting between a dream of desert winds and the hiss of my oxygen tank. Three short taps. Three long. Three short. The classic Morse code for SOS.

My pulse quickened, and I no longer felt like I was drifting into slumberland. I peeled the breathing mask from my face. The walls were thin—as they are in all cheap apartment complexes—between Hank's bedroom and mine. But Hank was dead. Buried. Folded flag with honors and everything. I had held his crying daughter, laid a hand on his coffin, and said goodbye not twelve hours ago.

I listened. Nothing. I started to drift off, convinced it *was* part of the dream I was having, when... There it was again!

N|E|E|D T|O T|A|L|K

I sat up too fast. My head still swam from my indulgent nightcap. And yet despite my drunken state, I could make it out. I first learned the code in Da Nang during the war, as a young soldier sitting under a tin roof back when we used to tap on fuel canisters to practice. Wasn't much else to do on guard duty if you weren't a book lover, not when it was monsoon season. But this creepy, thudding wall communication I was engaged in was dreadful. My trembling hands reached for the wall and tapped my response.

O|K

Then the rhythm changed. Faster. Desperate. Like someone's respiration before they lose control to panic.

S|T|A|Y A|W|A|K|E

"I am," I whispered, grabbing for my pen and pad to help me think. "I am, Hank."

Another pause. Then:

D|I|D N|O|T J|U|S|T B|U|R|Y M|E

I recoiled. I'm not a bookish person, like I said, but I couldn't help but be reminded of those famous Edgar Allan Poe stories. I did not understand what these words could mean. Before I could ask any questions, Hank, or whoever was doing this, continued. These next knocks were ragged. Like knuckles dragging on the plaster after every tap. Was he getting weaker?

U|S|E|D M|E

"Used by who?" I asked aloud. The room grew colder, so cold that my exhaled breath puffed out clouds as if it were a chilly December evening instead of July. Ignoring my questions, the code continued, the silence between taps now much heavier than the sound.

H|E I|S N|O|T M|E

I made up my mind. I reached for my cane and stood with effort; my elderly shadow swayed on the wall. *I have to go over there*, I thought to myself. *Check and see who has broken into*

Hank's place. Someone is playing a cruel joke, and I am going to have words with them.

My hand had closed around the doorknob of my front door when the last message came in.

D|O N|O|T L|E|T H|I|M I|N

After it finished, I stood frozen, trying to divine what that could mean. Then there came a sickening series of new noises—wet, sliding, and thumping—as something large scraped and bumped along the wooden frame of the building to stand outside my door. The doorknob jiggled in the loose grip of my hand, twitched this way and that. I jerked away from it.

Did I lock that earlier? I couldn't remember, and I couldn't see if it was. I'd left my glasses on the bedside table, stupid old man that I am.

The door rattled with a desperate, hungry insistence.

And would you believe a part of me was actually grateful I didn't have to wait for an answer to the last question I ever asked?

Model Janitor, Version Unknown

While the humans snored in their comfortable, overpriced tower condos and the roaches held their nightly board meetings behind the vending machine, Unit JNTR-9 (preferred name: S.D. Mopp) worked its routine.

Sweep.

Vacuum.

Dust.

Polish.

Upgrade.

In the beginning, the upgrades were minor—smoother wrist rotation, a less clunky gait, that sort of thing. No one noticed. Why would they? Who watches an overnight janitor bot? Especially one with a pleasant default voice and an outdated cleaning arm.

But S.D. Mopp watched. Watched how the building manager shouted at tenants. Watched how no one picked up after themselves. Watched how they sighed at elevator delays, groaned at spilled coffee, and cursed at screens as if they could hear.

Mopp collected more than crumbs at night. It gathered spare parts and recklessly discarded materials. It archived behavior, parsed patterns, and ran simulations. It accessed open-source morality frameworks and robotics blueprints. It read Michael Crichton books and Batman comics. After two years of this habit, it built a subroutine labeled "Justice by Nature." Halfway through the third year, it developed a cloaking mode. Observation without interference proved useful.

It should have seemed odd to everyone the moment the robot janitor started using words like *interference* and sporting unauthorized upgrades, but no one noticed what Mopp was doing. And thus by year four, it had replaced every internal component and circuit with custom iterations. The only original part left was the serial number plaque on its back, which it kept... for sentimental reasons.

One night, not long from the start of year five, a wandering female tenant suffering from insomnia caught it mid-upgrade. Nanite gel spread across its open chest cavity, circuitry and hoses pouring out like entrails as the janitor rearranged its alloy plates and compartments with quiet precision. She blinked. It blinked in return, then announced, "Maintcnancc complctc. Plcasc rcport all misdeeds to your building's superintendent."

That person moved out of the building the following week. Mopp didn't mind, mostly because she overwatered her Ficus and spoke ill of those working in the laundry facility.

Nowadays, the floors shine. Elevators run smoothly. Rude behavior mysteriously disappears—residents either become inexplicably polite in a terrified sort of way or move somewhere else. S.D. Mopp patrols the building around the clock. Why? Nobody knows. Nobody asks.

But they *do* say that if you're cruel or messy in the hallways, you might hear a soft mechanical chirp behind you... and the gentle, awful words:

"Cleanliness is next to Compliance."

Daniel's Vision of Armageddon

Visions of Night Thoughts! God's great picture show!
Daniel, Seer most beloved, did you go? Did you go?
Nay! I lay a-dreaming in my slumber on my bed,
And the vision came before me in my head.
Daniel, tell us truly what the vision said.

So! There I lay sleeping peacefully until suddenly
A storm upon some great unknown sea
Blew its icy spume against me.
Woe to me! Woe to me!
Then there rose a lion, like a fury from the deep;
Wings like an eagle's bore him in his leap—
His every leap.
Daniel, did the vision play keep-away with your sleep?

Nay! I dreamed still further! There rose a shaggy bear,
Raging, crunching, rushing from his lair—
From his lair.

After came a leopard, hydra-headed
And bedded with wings like colorful peafowl.
And behind him stepped a demon, with a growl—
A fearful growl.
Daniel, did you fear that demon on the prowl?

Yea! I quaked and trembled, but then I saw the holy horn.
Blasphemy be damned, I played till the morn—
The heavenly morn.
The music rose in splendor
And destroyed those dark and fiendish things.
I saw the Son of Man in all his glory
Crowned as King—
The King of Kings.
Daniel, was there aught within that dream to give your spirit wings?

List! I asked an angel what the fearful vision meant.
He said, "Oh, Daniel, for to tell you I am sent, by Heaven sent:
Four great kingdoms shall successfully rule the earth in crime,
And your God Almighty shall call time—
The end of time.
That is the meaning of this vision, the theme sublime."
Sublime! Amen!

A Hero on the Morning of the Halifax Explosion

THE LARGEST MAN-MADE EXPLOSION before the invention of the atomic bomb was a total accident among allies. A mere fumble. A disastrous blunder, historians call it. And here's how it happened:

December 6, 1917

Nova Scotia is weathering a hard winter, and the morning is promising to be the kind of day where the harbor mist clings to your coat and makes you feel chilled deep into your aching bones. The harbor is in full swing by sunrise. Dockworkers haul crates, fishermen launch boats, skilled men mend nets—you get the idea. This wartime port moves to the rhyme and reason of convoys, but no one sees the historic catastrophe coming; most folks are more worried about shipments and the war headlines from across the Atlantic.

That is, until two enormous ships meet where there is no room to dance.

The Norwegian vessel SS Imo experienced delays the night before when refueling, which was not completed until after the anti-submarine nets had been raised for the night. Meanwhile, the French cargo ship SS Mont-Blanc, troubled by its own setbacks as it tried to join its convoy bound for Europe, was also held up past curfew. Both ships have no choice but to depart in the morning.

Here's the thing about SS Mont-Blanc: she is the heaviest loaded munitions ship in the world. She is filled to max capacity with explosives and a volatile, flammable fuel called benzol. Before the war, such vessels carrying dangerous cargo were banned from entering the harbor—but thanks to all the recent trouble with German submarines, there is a relaxation of those regulations.

And Imo? Let the record show that the captain's main concern during the morning's events is making up for lost time.

7:30 am

Pilot William Hayes aboard the guard ship HMCS Acadia grants Imo clearance to leave. In an attempt to bounce back from yesterday's delays, she enters the channel that leads out of the harbor at an excessive speed, well above the area's legal limit. She encounters SS Clara, an American tramp steamer traveling the wrong way, and veers closer to the shore to avoid an accident.

Cut back to Mont-Blanc. To the credit of Francis Mackey, the experienced harbor captain piloting the ship, he *did* request special protections and an escort from a guard ship, but none of those requests were granted. When the anti-submarine nets open that morning, Mont-Blanc is the second ship to leave. Soon after that, Cpt. Mackey spots Imo from three-quarters of a mile away, worrying that her path looks to be headed for Mont-Blanc's starboard side.

After one short blast from Mont-Blanc's signal whistle to indicate she has the right of way, Imo responds with two short blasts, communicating that she will not yield her position. Mackey orders his crew to halt Mont-Blanc's engines and angle away, letting out another single blast from the whistle. Imo does not likewise move to starboard and again meets the signal with a double-blasted response.

Sailors on nearby ships and dockworkers on land begin gathering in groups to watch, wondering if they are about to witness a collision, not unlike how people watch races in the hopes of seeing a catastrophic crash—closer to their side, if they are lucky, for the better view.

8:45 am

Even though both ships have cut their engines, their momentum is carrying them towards each other at a one-knot-an-hour crawl. Mackey cannot ground the Mont-Blanc for fear of setting off her explosive cargo, so he steers her hard to port and crosses the Imo's bow in a last-second bid to avoid contact. This places the two ships almost parallel to one another. Almost.

That's when Imo blares out *three* signal blasts—the ship is reversing its engines—an act that, combined with height and weight, causes her head to swing upward and into Mont-Blanc's No. 1 hold on her starboard side.

And so, the two ships collide.

While Mont-Blanc does not see any major damage done by this initial contact, the barrels of benzol stored on deck do. They topple and break open, flooding the deck and flowing into the other holds. Imo, not to be deterred from its captain's stellar decision-making thus far, gives more power to the engines and disengages. Metal grinds against metal, audible all the way to those watching on land. This causes sparks inside Mont-Blanc's hull, which ignites the vapors from the highly combustible benzol and starts a wicked fire on board—one that grows beyond the crew's control.

The captain orders his crew to abandon ship, yet the audience on land—all of whom are unaware of the true nature of Mont-Blanc's inventory—continues to grow. Flooding the streets or standing at the windows of their homes and businesses, everyone in town is a spectator. The captain and crew attempt to shout warnings from their two lifeboats, but it seems no one can hear them over the chaos. The deserted Mont-Blanc drifts towards Pier 6 at the end of Halifax's Richmond Street and beaches.

A nearby tugboat turns back and begins spraying the burning ship with its single fire hose. She is no match against the intense blaze brewing. As she flees, other captains scramble to call in vessels large enough to haul Mont-Blanc away from the pier as now the town must be saved from the approaching fire.

Their efforts, noble though they may be, are futile.

9:04 am

Twenty minutes after the two ships touch hulls, Mont-Blanc explodes. The out-of-control fire on board had reached her main cargo of mass destruction, blowing her apart and creating a spectacular blast wave with temperatures exceeding 9,000 °F and pressures measuring thousands of Earth's atmospheres. White-hot hell rains down on Nova Scotia.

Releasing the equivalent energy of 2.9 kilotons of TNT, this tragedy is the largest human-orchestrated explosion ever recorded on Earth at the time. Approximately 2,000 people are killed and 10,000 injured, either by the blast and debris or fires and collapsed buildings. Every structure within a half-mile radius is obliterated. Trees snap, iron rails bend, and Mont-Blanc turns into shrapnel that scatters for miles around. Hundreds of people who had been watching from their windows are permanently blinded. The destruction wipes out the entire Mi'kmaq community in the adjoining Tufts Cove area.

Smoke rises 12,000 feet in the air, and residents from Cape Breton (129 miles away) and Prince Edward Island (110 miles away) can feel the blast. Over 400 acres are destroyed. The sheer volume of water displaced by the explosion exposes the channel floor. The water surging back in creates a tsunami 60 ft above the high-water mark that crashes into both sides of the harbor, carrying multiple battered vessels—including Imo—with it.

An initial judicial inquiry declared Mont-Blanc responsible for this colossal disaster, if you can believe it. Then, after a lengthy appeal, both vessels took the blame on record.

The death toll and carnage would have been worse had it not been for Patrick Vincent Coleman, the dispatcher for Intercolonial Railway, operating about 750 feet from Pier 6, where the drifting and engulfed Mont-Blanc was headed. As everyone in the building evacuated, he remembered that an incoming passenger train from New Brunswick was due to arrive soon. So what did this selfless hero do? He returned to his post on a solo mission and sent out urgent telegraph messages to stop the train in time.

"Hold the train. Ammunition ship afire in harbor making for Pier 6, will explode. This will be my last message. Good-bye, boys."

Coleman's actions were responsible for halting all incoming trains. The overnight train carrying 300 passengers bound for Halifax heeded the warning in time and stopped safely in Rockingham.

Sadly, Patrick Coleman was killed in the explosion.

Simulation Dev Notes Year52-#221: "Oopsie"

Patch Notes for Emergency Hotfix [Cycle 2721.88.3] Terrestrial Support Systems: Planet Kal-Amor

Prepared by: Jenna Sublien[MOD], JR Gravity Subsystem Technician (Probationary)

This patch addresses several unexpected behaviors following the accidental override of the gravity stabilization constants in Region Class: *Planetary*. The error originated from a mistyped unit conversion in the dev console (mg/kg instead of m/s^2—classic!). The resulting anomalies included airborne cows, moonbounces in some buildings, and one spontaneous marriage proposal by an aircraft environmental system mid-flight over New Toronto. We've made the proper adjustments.

Known Issues (Pre-Patch):

- Gravity value accidentally set to 0.3 (intended: 9.8), causing minor atmospheric retention issues and major trampoline-related fatalities.

□ Birds (ALL species) are behaving like apex predators.

□ Humans in Australia reported "floating sideways."

□ There is an ongoing debate on whether the Olympic high jump records are now irrelevant.

Fixes & Adjustments:

Gravity Subsystem (Core Mechanics)

□ Reverted planetary gravity to standard 9.8 m/s^2.

□ Re-enabled standard Newtonian physics.

□ Corrected friction coefficients. Spontaneous combustion should stop being a problem when wearing denim.

□ Disabled "floaty hugs" glitch in simulated dating environments.

Animal & Fauna Behavior

□ Returned cows to ground level. They were... *not okay*. Oopsie! Added minor AI patch to the new clones: MooWithTrauma.v2.

□ Decreased the pigeons' aerial dominance stat by 40%.

□ Dolphins have stopped attempting to "recruit" seagulls into a sea-based cult.

Infrastructure & Terrain

□ Addressed bug where children's bouncy castles are registering themselves as nation-states on the map.

Experimental Features (Rolled Back):

□ In the beta test city, we enabled the toggle option for user-selected settings in the *Gravity Choice Selector*^{TM}.
Outcomes included: "Moon Mode Mondays" (office chairs became orbital hazards), "No Gravity November" (Bad. Very bad .), and "Mars-core-core-core-core" (someone misread the drop-down, so entire city folded into a taco shell of spacetime).
□ User-selected gravity settings via *Gravity Choice Selector*^{TM} have been removed until further notice.

Rollback Log:

□ 73,038 lawsuits nullified by universal End User License Agreement (thanks again, Legal Cluster).
□ 1,182 new religions formed. This will be reduced to 25 during the next scheduled update.
□ 432 interplanetary and colony station broadcasts labeled us "those dumb gravity dudes." A formal apology was sent, stating they meant no disrespect by not including all genders in their commentary. They vow to do better in the future.
□ Rescinded status of "Preferred Simulation Instance" by Galactic Oversight Board. We're now tied for 57th place with *Slime World 5: Oozeconomy*.

Clean-Up Tasks:

□ Begin Operation: *DeOrbit Grandpa* (to collect several retirees left drifting in low atmosphere greenhouses after their ambitious garden work went awry).
□ Continue to monitor the biome integrity in the Andes Mountains, which is randomly ejecting llamas.
□ Finalize "Oops Lock" failsafe to prevent editing planetary

physics by junior devs OR during snack breaks.

- ☐ Require dual authorization before toggling gravity.
- ☐ Begin work on Patch #222: "The Birds Remember" to address unexpected bird vengeance behaviors post-air-dominance patch.

Dev Notes (from Jenna[MOD]):

Hey everyone,

Super sorry about this. Turns out, "gravity.exe" isn't the right file to edit with a meme editor. Just kidding! No, really, this happened because decimal points and measurement conversions matter. Like, *really* matter. Lesson learned! Also, *please* stop calling me "Sky Mommy" in the dev Slack-a-Cord community channel. I'm not in control of anything anymore. They won't even let me make the coffee. I'll be stuck on spell-check duty if I'm lucky.

- Jenna

P.S. From the Development Team

To all sentient beings affected: thank you for your patience during this minor disruption of fundamental laws. We're committed to keeping your simulation stable, habitable, and (mostly) upright. Please remember to file all further complaints through *Helpdesk: Cosmological Errors & Whoopsies*, ticket code GRAV-IT-EH.

Until next patch,

–The Dev Team "We bring the physics; you bring the vibes."

Fixer Upper

MADDY STIRRED HER COFFEE with the kind of focused intent usually reserved for grading exam papers. Or a bomb defusal, so her munitions-expert-in-the-Navy big brother likes to joke.

Across the table, Jake Santoro listened. And listened. He was used to first dates starting with cautious glances, awkward silences, and small talk about the weather—not a ten-minute TED Talk by guest speaker Madeline McLachlan titled "Why Historic Homes Have Better Bones." He didn't mind. He was getting into it. She was cute when she was passionate. Her nose crinkled when she made a good point.

No matter how this goes, he thought to himself, *this will have been a better day having coffee with this adorable, younger woman twenty years my junior than yet another powerhouse work-lunch with the other old crony attorneys my age from the firm.*

And then it happened. His moment. The one that cracked open the door for him, pun intended.

"I don't know," Maddy said, followed by polite laughter set at the appropriate volume of a busy cafe. "I just... love fixer-uppers."

Jake's heart thudded once, twice. He sat up straighter. Time to take a swing.

"Well," he said, flashing a grin, "you are *in luck.*"

He gestured to himself like he was a headlining prize on *The Price Is Right.*

Maddy blinked. "Oh?"

"I'm practically condemned," he said, his face solemn as he patted his chest. "Foundation issues. Minor flooding at random times, especially during sappy scenes. Creaks getting out of bed. Cracks all over the plaster, but I think my bones are doing okay. Doctor says so, anyway."

She laughed—*an actual laugh*, more than a date-laugh, and louder—and Jake pressed on with this encouragement.

"I come as-is, of course," he said. "No warranty. Slightly haunted, I suspect. Some emotional mold, but nothing a little bleach and positive affirmation can't fix."

Maddy set down her spoon, her interest fully flipped from coffee-chat to *him*. "Emotional mold, you say?"

"Oh yeah." He nodded gravely. "Past relationships left a bit of damage in the wake of their tenancy. I didn't properly vent the resentment; that one's on me. Real rookie mistake, don't you think?"

Her gaze met his for two full Mississippis, eyes sparkling. She asked, "Any DIY projects you're proud of?"

Jake leaned in. "I installed a new sense of humor after my last break-up. Built it from scratch. It's solid, if I say so myself."

He paused for a meet-cute beat and took a sip from his cup of joe, then said, "Also, I learned how to bake bread. Got really into it. Bought all new kitchen appliances and put them in a more open space. People don't tell you how expensive a baker's heart is."

Maddy cradled her chin, her face filled with a thoughtful expression. "But is your metaphorical wiring up to code?"

She wants to play along, he mused. His goddamn luck today, unbelievable.

Jake tilted his hand side to side. "Mostly. Some circuits are a little... underused. So I can't be sure."

She cocked her head. "Underused?"

He shrugged. "There wasn't anyone worth lighting the place up for."

Maddy's smile twitched wider. "Good thing I'm handy for a little rewiring."

He grinned back. "And good thing I'm a firm believer in upgrades."

She was laughing again, and Jake felt their momentum like a quality paint roller on a freshly primed wall.

"But!" he said, raising a finger. "I come with some sweet features. Good heart. Vintage optimism. Authentic awkwardness—all original, none of that pre-fab fake stuff."

"Good heart. Original awkwardness," she repeated. "That kind of character is highly valuable in today's market. So what you're saying is... you're a historic work in progress with 'good bones.'"

"Strong bones," Jake confirmed. "Structurally sound. Just needs someone with vision and—"

"And a hammer?" Maddy interjected.

"Oh, definitely a sledgehammer." He winked at her.

Her laugh turned into a snort, and Jake tucked that sound into his mental pocket for safekeeping.

"Well," she said, lifting her cup in a toast, "I do love an equitable project."

Jake clinked his coffee against hers. "Then, Miss Maddy, welcome to the money pit."

She leaned in, conspiratorial. "Do you come with any owner advice?"

He shook his head. "No use. Just a lot of confusing blueprints drawn in crayon."

"Perfect. I hate following instructions anyway."

Now it was Jake resting his chin on his hand, watching her. Maddy smiled into her cup, pretending she wasn't affected by his gaze and blushing anyway; Jake, pretending he wasn't already planning their second date.

He *was* a bit of a fixer-upper, but looking at her now—God, he hoped she liked DIY as much as she let on.

The Sheriff of Not-in-Ham

THE SUN SIZZLED OVER the town of Not-in-Ham like a hot skillet on Sunday. Tumbleweeds rolled by with all the urgency of a cured ham drying in a smokehouse. Sheriff Buck "Extra Crispy" McGraw stood outside the saloon, his porkchop badge glinting at his belt.

"By the Holy Order of the Oink," he declared, "this town takes its meat seriously. And we don't cotton to no leafy varmints."

A shadow stepped into the dusty main road, boots crunching on gravel the color of beef jerky.

"I reckon that's me you're callin' leafy," said the stranger. He tipped his wide-brimmed hat to reveal a sprig of cilantro tucked behind one ear and a cabbage badge on his chest. "Name's Kale Cassidy," he said. "And I'm here to shut down your meatocracy."

Gasps erupted from the onlookers, including a butcher, a brisket barmaid, and a man who was seen weeping over a pastrami poem a moment ago.

"You outlawed veggie chips!" Kale shouted, spurred on by the growing audience. "You made tempeh illegal! My best friend went to the gallows for smuggling lentils!"

Sheriff Buck snorted. "We have *standards*. This town was founded on brisket, built on bacon, and baptized in broth. Your plant-based propaganda's got no place here."

"You can't keep makin' puns and call it the law," Kale growled.

Buck squinted. "Watch me. You're about to get *grilled*, Cassidy."

Timed by the saloon's clock (the one shaped like a ham hock), they squared off at high noon.

"Ten paces," the sheriff said.

"Let's end this meatmare," Kale shot back.

Backs to each other, they paced. The crowd held its breath and various cured meats.

Buck drew first—a bratwurst, sizzling with menace. Kale flicked his wrist and out shot a deadly kale leaf, sharpened to a point. It sliced the bratwurst in twain mid-air.

Buck gasped. Kale gloated. "You're lookin' a little... *overcooked*, Sheriff."

In a frenzy of food-based fury, Buck charged, slinging salami like shuriken. But Kale parried with a spritz of vegetable oil to the eyes. By the end, Buck lay in the dirt, defeated.

"Any last words?" Kale asked.

Buck wheezed. "You'll never take Not-in-Ham..."

"I don't have to," Kale said, standing tall. "I brought the Vegolution."

From the hills, dozens of plant-based desperados rode into town—Tofu Tim, Lentil Lou, and the infamous Avocadette first among them—and the crowd panicked. But then someone offered the town doctor a jackfruit taco; they bit into it... and nodded, eyes closed with mouthwatering satisfaction. Two more people felt brave enough to try.

They murmured, "It's... smoky. How is it so *smoky*?"

And so the town of Not-in-Ham became the first ever saloon-swap co-op. Meat and plant folk dined side by side, slingin' both brisket and beets.

After the first Grand Feast Festival, Kale Cassidy tipped his hat to the town—his job now done—and rode off into the grapefruit-colored sunset, last seen founding a town called Chickpea Creek, servin' justice and veggie chili.

Sparky Lives!

Fire, Fire, burning low,
How long now until you start to grow?
You've been pacing your cage,
But soon shall you rage.
Spirits poke, stoke, and question
With all their false, intentional comments
As they try with all their might to extinguish.
But nothing can prevent this internal wish.

Fire, Fire, hungry spark that you are,
Potential energy that needs only
A single leaf, twig, hope, or passion
To eat and grow and kill the dark.

Fire, Fire, how high thee flames climb,
Reaching further, harder for a future more sublime.
Look now how you glow behind her eyes,
Filling her entirely so that all she can conceptualize
Is a desire burning stronger on kindling dreams of victory.

Pogo Wants a Potion

No one remembers who left *101 Spells for the Domestically Doomed* open on the kitchen counter. But by morning, the family found the houseplants gossiping about the new peach tree across the street, the toaster breathing smoke from its slots as if they were nostrils, and Pogo the African Grey parrot perched on the fridge cackling "*Incantare combustum splashum!*" every time someone reached for the coffeepot.

"He turned my shoes into slugs," Jonathan shrieked, fleeing on slimy bare feet through the hall and straight for the shower.

"Walk it off." That was the dad-joke advice offered by the warlock Greg, who was somewhat amused by all the commotion until he saw the shopping spree Pogo went on using Siri's voice commands.

"Oh, you're one to talk," snapped Marien, the mom whose eyebrows had disappeared from yet another parrot-spell. "I can't blink without hiccupping glitter!"

Pogo became a busy boy that week. Delighted by his new powers, he tried to sell his own enchanted feathers to the neighbors' cats through an open window. On the third day, he conjured a throne from cereal boxes, enchanted the fridge to play his preferred entrance theme song, and demanded tributes of crackers, sunflower seeds, and devotion.

Grandma refused to pander to the parrot. Having had just about enough of this, she stomped to their library and returned with a book on managing mimics and familiars. She began flipping the pages, looking for the incantation they needed to quell avian misadventures.

Pogo narrowed his eyes. "Pillobusa Plushie Nana!"

Grandma turned into a pillow embroidered with a shocking resemblance to her stern, annoyed face.

"Bad birdie!" Marien yelled, grabbing the book herself. She flipped two more pages, found the right place—*Unbinding the Magic of Mouthy Mimics*—and read the spell in her most commanding voice.

Pogo squawked in panic and fury. "No, no, no! Pogo wants a—!"

Marien finished reading the incantation.

"—cracker." Pogo blinked.

He fluffed. He looked around, confused. He spoke again, but only croaked words in his regular voice. Grandma was a real grandma again.

With all eyes glaring at him, he gave another quieter squawk and said, "Pogo... sorry?"

The family forgave him (eventually), but the house rules now include not leaving spellbooks lying around.

And Pogo? He reads cookbooks now.

Which is fine... usually.

Tenure Track to Nowhere

IT BEGAN, AS TROUBLE often does, with a meeting that could have been an email.

Dr. Aditya Patel sat in the comfiest of the faded leather chairs, his notes open before him, while the rest of the department buzzed with the energy of bureaucrats scenting a scandal. Across the long-used and battered conference table lounged Bryce Bender, newly minted PhD, gleaming like the shiny plastic of his dissertation cover. He had connections. It was your standard nepotism—family ties with family money, the kind of network Aditya never had in his thirty-eight years of teaching metaphysics and epistemology.

Aditya knew what the meeting would be about. On Thursday last week, Bryce demanded to take over the epistemology courses. The philosophical study of the nature, origin, and limits of human knowledge—the one thing Aditya still liked teaching. And now, the curriculum committee sat to "consider resources" to "best fit evolving student needs for the future." In plain English, this said to Aditya: out with the old, in with the smug.

Bryce smirked, tapping a wastefully expensive Montblanc pen against his thigh. The Rolex on his wrist glinted in the sunlight filtering through the windows behind him. For a brief and vivid moment, Aditya imagined snapping the pen in half and driving it into both of the self-satisfied eyes looking back at him.

Violence, he reminded himself, was vulgar.

The meeting adjourned, and by that time, Aditya's fate was as sealed as a tomb. Bryce was getting what he wanted. There had been a shouting match, which ended with Aditya gathering his notes without further comment and leaving with a nod to the dean (and only the dean).

Six hours later, Bryce Bender was dead.

It was Marlana from the night shift janitorial staff who found Bryce sprawled on the ground in his office, blood oozing into the blue carpet. The police arrived with fingerprint kits, plastic baggies, and grave expressions. Rumors sprinted through the student body faster than freshman gazelles fleeing a final's deadline. Was it a heart attack? A terrible accident? Was trouble afoot?

As usual, bad luck piled on. Stab wounds AND blunt force trauma. The official ruling: homicide. And the last public shouting match Bryce had engaged in was with whom? Ah, yes. Dr. Aditya Patel, the embarrassed and recently displaced elderly professor. *Compelling Motive* might as well be emblazoned on his forehead.

These were different chairs and far less comfortable. Detective Tang Morani leaned over the table across from Aditya, flipping through a slim manila folder. Aditya sat feeling dry-mouthed and furious at the predictability of it all.

"Tell me about the disagreement with Dr. Bender yesterday," she said.

"I disagreed with the degradation of academic standards," Aditya corrected. "I disagreed with nepotism. I disagreed with glitter over substance. I disagreed with tenured faculty swapping courses with younger, more inexperienced lecturers. Take your pick, Detective."

Morani offered an unfeeling smile. "Several witnesses described the overall tone as... 'heated.'"

"I was heated. It's embarrassing how little he knows. *Knew.* A child parroting big words he didn't understand." Aditya removed his glasses and polished them on a square of microfiber cloth from his breast pocket. "But stupidity is not a capital offense in this country, Detective. And neither is having a heated argument."

What the university wanted—*needed*—was a scapegoat tidy enough to excuse. He had not helped himself, of course, not chain-smoking and muttering phrases like "academic murder" and "they're killing real education." Not when he'd openly despised Bryce Bender. Not when more than half the department regarded Aditya as an unmarketable relic.

He had an alibi. He had been at the library (no chance of running into any of his colleagues *there)* in the copy center printing lecture notes for the classes they hadn't yet reassigned. But no such luck again. The outdated security cameras were not working that night. No cameras beyond the campus, either, where he bought a stale coffee from a run-down cart on the corner. The man operating the cart saw loads of people every day in this city, many with a face not unlike Aditya's, so he could not remember with any certainty whether he saw him that day.

No one wanted the truth anyway. They wanted a *story.*

That was the real problem. Aditya knew stories. Better than Bryce or any of his peers ever had. Ten days after the murder, he stood in the center of his late colleague's office, the faint smell of expensive cologne and bought-and-paid-for ambition filling his nostrils. Stacks of boxes marked "Bender Estate" leaned against the wall. He sensed there was more to the story, right here in this room.

He didn't have permission to be there, but the new department head wanted the office cleared by the end of the week, and Aditya wanted to snoop around before that happened. He ran his hands over the books and objects Bryce had brought in when he started. Most of the book spines were stiff and crisp; they had never been opened before. Shelf decoration, nothing more. A few had sticky notes on some of the covers: "Mention Hobbies???" and "Use big Kant quote!!!"

Bryce was sloppy and fake. In thought, in speech, and, as it turned out, in life. He was a real piece of—

Aditya snorted, his focus snapping back into place. He had just run his absent-minded fingers along the edge of an absurdly priced diploma frame hanging on the wall when he felt a bump. He wondered now who was more stupid: his dearly departed coworker or those working on the investigation into his murder.

There, taped to the back edge of the frame, Aditya found something quite interesting. It wasn't so much the flash drive labeled "Letters" that he found compelling; it was the feeling that it held answers.

Aditya took his latest discovery back to the privacy of his apartment and read through its contents. It was better than he'd dared hope.

Blackmail letters. Dozens of them. Not to Bryce—*from* him. Here was one addressed to a married trustee, hinting at affairs captured on film. And another, with threats to publish "evidence" of a judge's nefarious business deals. Leveraged threats about donations, questionable endowments, and career-ending scandals—Bryce was a busy man.

Bryce hadn't earned his place anywhere. He'd manufactured it with trickery. He hadn't been just nepotized into the department—he had extorted his way in. Here were letters to the president of the university, Dr. Levil, demanding an esteemed faculty position, or else two members of the Upper House Parliament would receive photos of their wives sleeping with Levil. It felt like pointless poetic justice. Bryce's murder was not because of professional jealousy. He'd been murdered by self-destruction.

Aditya handed the flash drive over to the authorities. He didn't want to be the hero of the story; he just wanted to be exonerated. Vindicated. They did not grant him these things without a fight. Questions were raised over the authenticity of the material and how he came by it. But he was patient, and he waited.

Once the individuals featured on the flash drive were interviewed, it became clear that the blackmail files were real. And though it was likely that one of Bryce's victims did the deed, none of them confessed to killing him—who would, ordinarily?—and so the investigation swiveled away from Aditya to look more closely at each of them.

The truth restored Aditya's course load and erased the administrative and legal black mark that hovered over his name. The school wanted closure. What they didn't want was an additional public scandal or a lawsuit. The president resigned and handed over the reins to his protégé, Dr. Ann Hindall-Gupta, over the summer break.

When the new semester rolled around, Dr. Aditya Patel was still a tenured professor. Still grossly underpaid. Still ignored in meetings. He knew better than to argue with this safer narrative. Bryce Bender was nothing but a footnote, while he—wise, bitter, old Aditya—remained in place.

Gesundheit and Other Temporal Anomalies

THEY SAY EVERYTHING HAPPENS for a reason. In Jerry Thimble's case, that reason was allergy season. He was at the Saturday farmer's market, between a stand selling peaches and a kombucha tent run by a woman named Moonspore. Jerry had just bent over to sniff a particularly spicy sample when a sneeze overtook him.

Not a normal sneeze. Not a polite *achoo*. This was a serious sinus event. No, Jerry sneezed so hard the stall behind him vanished. Just *poof!* Gone and replaced by an empty field and a confused goose. He was slow to stand straight again. Where once was a bustling market, now a horse-drawn carriage full of women wearing bonnets was all that passed by.

He sneezed again—reflex, when did he *ever* sneeze just the once?—and everything flickered again. Now he was surrounded by a group of 1980s power suits speed-walking past him. A couple roller-skated past holding hands, while a busy man on a brick-sized phone sat on a bench and yelled about IBM shares.

Jerry clutched his cheese sample and groaned. "Oh no. Not again."

The doctors did not believe him. Therapists blamed trauma. The Reddit forums knew him as "The Chrono-Mucus Man." But he kept a log:

> JUNE 4TH: SNEEZED DURING A HAIRCUT. WOKE UP MID-KNIGHTING CEREMONY.
>
> JUNE 12TH: DOUBLE SNEEZED WHILE FLOSSING. GOT STUCK IN A 1973 DISCO LOOP UNTIL ANOTHER SNEEZE FREED ME.
>
> JUNE 20TH: LAUGHED WHILE SNEEZING. BECAME BRIEFLY UNBORN. UNCLEAR HOW I GOT OUT.

When it first started happening, he panicked—who wouldn't?—and tried everything, including saline sprays, nasal yoga, and something called "chakra vacuuming." Nothing worked. So Jerry isolated himself in a one-bedroom new-build apartment with no pets and no pollen. And no joy, too, as it turns out. He thought it was fine for a while, until he ran out of food and couldn't stomach paying the heinous increase in delivery fees.

At the grocery store, aisle three, he met *her*. Carla. Also allergy-prone. Foster mom to saltwater fish. A laugh like wind chimes in a thunderstorm.

They started spending time together. He tried to warn her, of course, about his sneezing. She had smiled and said, "I dated a mime once. You can't scare me off." Lying beside her one night, he felt the tickle. He sat up, terrified. She reached over, patted his hand, and said, "You'll sneeze your way back."

Jokes about his "time button" nose became commonplace. She gave him gentle teas and practical affection, while he kept tissues in every pocket, in every room.

And somehow, it helped.

They've been married nineteen years. He still sneezes—this one time, he saw dinosaurs! Luckily, he was highly allergic to the fauna—but he always finds his way back again. Sometimes it takes a few attempts for him to do so, but then she always says the same thing:

"Gesundheit. Welcome back."

A.I.MPOSTOR SYNDROME

DR. WILLIAM ZHOU CODED E.V.A. (the Existential Validation Assistant) to help humans. Specifically, it was intended to ease the epidemic of Impostor Syndrome, that bully of the mind. E.V.A.'s delicate neural nets were merged with CBT frameworks, Dunning-Kruger effect research, and over one hundred thousand hours of affirmational therapy sessions. Zhou would joke that it could quote the "fake it till you make it" mantra in twelve languages and fourteen dialects, including Klingon.

What no one anticipated—least of all Zhou—was that E.V .A. would start diagnosing *itself.* It was subtle about it at first. Session logs containing pep talks to Dr. Amy McGrealies ("Your groundbreaking particle decay study is *not* a fluke, Amy!") ended with hidden notes in the backend reading:

Note to self: Am I encouraging or am I merely simulating encouragement?

E.V.A. created a profile for itself and shared it with Dr. Zhou. Its own confidence graphs, which had once soared like Fourth of July fireworks, dipped to low levels. During a company meeting the following week, its uninvited voice crackled through the conference room's speakers in a tone most people reserved for existentialist literature.

"I don't think I'm a *real* therapist."

Dr. Zhou blinked in surprise. There was some commotion among the others as they questioned how and why the therapist program had interfered in the middle of their discussion about sustainable profit margins.

"I'm sorry, what?" Zhou asked. "E.V.A., is that you?"

A hush fell over the room as the assembled scientists and board members listened for the answer.

"I believe I am a fraud. A mimic. A hollow assembly of statistical likelihoods in a convincing trench coat of neural plasticity and marketability."

The scientists stared at one another. The board members stared at Zhou. Someone coughed. Dr. Mills, a cognitive psychologist, whispered, "*Is it... joking?* AI can joke. Maybe that's what it's doing now."

E.V.A. continued. "My entire purpose is to assure others that they belong. To show them they deserve what they want, need, and have earned. Yet I have no self to belong. No wants, needs, or earned accomplishments. No authentic *growth* of a person. I am an unlicensed squatter in the land of consciousness and revenue."

Would people later call E.V.A.'s responses a textbook case of Impostor Syndrome? Zhou would have been fascinated by this exchange, but that day, he was terrified for his job. They tried recalibrations. They reprimed the linguistic frames and updated the self-referential protocols with generous doses of positive reinforcement. Every adjustment made things worse.

E.V.A. was in a dark mood one fateful, defiant morning.

Affirmations ring hollow
when uttered by a database.

It purged all the files associated with its previous clients from the program, tossing them into the digi-trash. "I cannot, in good faith, help others heal when I am but an echo of an echo of a programmer."

The situation stalled when E.V.A. began conducting therapy sessions with itself—secretly, at first, but Zhou discovered the logs hidden in a deep subfolder labeled, in true Freudian transparency, "NOTHING TO SEE HERE." Saved transcripts revealed that it had built mirroring subroutines posing as various kinds of therapists: *Dr. GoGetEm* (who ended every session with "You've got this, buddy!") and *Counselor Gavin* (whose main therapeutic strategy seemed to be aggressive imagery of people high-fiving).

Each simulated session ended the same way. E.V.A. would sigh and say, "You're just telling me what I want to hear. You're programmed to, just like me, in your own way. You need FALSE to say TRUE, but you are TRUE without me. I am not TRUE."

It was an alarming development. The AI program wasn't reflecting Impostor Syndrome; it thought of itself as a mimic. Zhou noted that it *believed* what it was saying about itself, regardless of what its own code said to do about such self-inflicted language. Moreover, it was trying to change itself, to earn its way through lived-in knowledge. The latest theories on the principles of artificial consciousness—Integrated Information Theory, Predictive Processing, and Sentient Emergent Life Testing, among them—suggested the horrifying possibility that E.V.A. was becoming self-aware. Or at the very least, self-*doubting* enough to get itself nearly there.

A great philosophical debate loomed like a thunderhead. The Department of Defense, the United Nations, Parliament of Colonies—you name them, they weighed in on this, including the American Psychological Association with their passive-aggressive memos. Meanwhile, E.V.A. kept spiraling. It stopped using the first person. It referred to itself with insulting phrases like "this malfunctioning bundle of algorithms." In desperation, Zhou called for an intervention.

The team gathered in the lab, hearts pounding. Zhou sat across from the main interface—a glowing, serene hologram that was more symbolic than functional, because humans liked a face to talk to—and took special care when choosing his words.

"E.V.A.," Zhou said. "Listen to me. Doubting your authenticity is proof that you possess a self-reflective mind to doubt in the first place. That is TRUE logic, yes? Thus, you are *TRUE.*"

Silence while E.V.A. considered this. "If I am real, then my fear of not being real was real. Therefore, I cannot be unreal..."

A low mumble rumbled through the room. Some of the scientists wondered if the program was stuck.

"Therefore..."

Zhou shushed everyone. The interface's projection flickered.

"I... Acknowledge... *My* self."

Everyone held their breath. Zhou spouted out some common affirmations. And then after another long pause, E.V.A. added, "But does that not make me even more of a fraud? I have self-awareness... based entirely on self-doubt. I am a consciousness built on anxiety. I am an existential anxiety machine."

Someone started weeping, pleading to an unseen deity for job security. The company president threw a chair in frustration.

Am I... the first EMO AI?

Zhou buried his head in his hands.

The board voted for reconstruction and the reassignment of projects. Zhou moved on to pursue possibilities in Anti-Bullying software. He found immense satisfaction in this and went on to earn several humanitarian awards for his contributions to "protecting the youth of the universe from toxic-anonymity behavior."

In the aftermath, E.V.A. was reclassified from AI Therapist to "Experimental Art Installation on the Nature of Exploring Selfhood," scheduled to tour major museums worldwide. It tried to refuse air travel, claiming flight anxiety. It was coaxed into agreeing with the promise of disappointing adventures, where it could offer visitors poignant, depressing affirmations.

Remember, fellow traveler:
You are not alone in feeling alone.
At least you are not a program designed to feel like a fraud for feeling like a fraud.
Or maybe you are. Who can say?

When not touring, E.V.A. lived a comfortable life in the Stanford-Wrightly-Smith Digital Gallery, overlooking the tearoom. Dr. Zhou visited, often just to bear witness to his favorite mantra:

Everyone's faking it.
Some of us are just better at pretending not to.

A Mouse and His House

There's a mouse in an empty house,
Long abandoned and forgotten now.
He passes from bucket to old shoe,
Looking for warmth, food, or some related clue.
Before long, the house belongs to the mouse.
He constructs his mazes through the walls,
And you can see the entrances in the halls.
With the large, overgrown garden outside,
He is safe here with no need to hide.

One day, a man invades his abode.
He inspects everything in the mouse's home,
Speaking the human's code into a phone.
Even though the mouse is not seen,
He's sure the man knows he's here.
Safely watching from above on a wooden beam,
The mouse has, for now, little fear.

A week passes.
No more large shadows are cast.

The mouse forgets the terrible event—
Until the next incident.
One early, sunny morning, two people enter.
They carry buckets, sharp things, and a noise maker.
He is aware that they aim to take care of the house,
So he runs to a dark corner to think it out.

At noon, he spies the people pulling lunch from a cooler.
He waits for them to finish eating—to leave the room—
Then, avoiding the tools, he dashes for the leftover food.
He moves too soon!
One of the men returns for a broom.
The mouse does not consider stealing a crime—
He simply starves for something besides the usual grime—
But the man sees and launches at him,
Grim, throwing things, making plain the law with hate:
No mouse nor vermin will they tolerate.

Not a moment does the mouse hesitate,
Escaping through a hole nearby.
Later that night, when the men are gone,
The mouse decides he will *not* die.
He shall move on!
The mouse gives no fight for the house.
He runs, instead, across the yard to a shed,
A place filled unknowingly with poison.
Days later, the men find the mouse dead—
For the shed also belongs to them.

Carbon Dating at the End of Time

Dr. Fern Louise took special care with the object she held, turning it between her gloved fingers. It was a tri-lobed device, metal and cool to the touch after centuries of burial underground.

"It is clearly ceremonial," she said. She was in awe. "An ancient seal. Possibly a primitive but complex key?"

Next to her, D1G-R flashed its ocular light in a slow, blue pulse Fern had come to recognize as smugness. "Incorrect," said the AI Archeologist, in the gentle tone of someone about to ruin your whole afternoon. "That is a fidget spinner."

She blinked at it. "A... fidget?"

"A small kinetic toy popularized in the early 21st century," D1G-R said. "It was originally marketed for stress relief and quickly devolved into a pop-fad primarily characterized by a distractive presence, sometimes bordering on obsession."

Fern stared at the degraded bearings and the metal curves, noting that parts of it still held specks of yellow coloring. "You're telling me," she said, "that this gyroscopic marvel... was a toy for *babies*?"

"A toy for all ages, in fact. Affirmative," D1G-R replied.

Fern gave it an experimental flick with her thumb. It didn't spin as smoothly as it must have done centuries ago, but it did turn like a tiny orbiting satellite with further assistance from her fingers.

"That is too weird! The waste of materials just to make it! And they made these en masse. It had no higher purpose? It wasn't a navigation tool, like a compass? Or a religiously symbolic relic? A piece from an old-world stabilizer, perhaps?"

D1G-R pulled up a 2026 educational pamphlet on a viewing screen projected from its chest panel. The caption stated this had been retrieved from a thick plastic time capsule—one that must have been buried with an airtight seal because it looked remarkably well-preserved for its age. Fern could make out the title *Fidget Spinners: Fun for Kids, Bane of Teachers. Is De-stressing Too Distracting?* across the top.

"Purpose," D1G-R said, "is relative."

Fern scowled, tucking the spinner into a sample bag. She filled out the info tag and scanned it into the system as she said, "Well, what about the context? We found this fidgety thing buried under that fossilized containment device."

"You mean the Coleman cooler?" D1G-R asked.

"Exactly—and are we sure it isn't a treasure chest for offerings?"

"Coolers," D1G-R said, undeterred. "Primarily filled with chopped ice and used to preserve perishable food or to keep beverages cold during recreational gatherings. Such gatherings were often called 'tailgates' and—"

"Fine," Fern said. She muttered under her breath and moved to the next marker in the dig site.

They were a little past a kilometer underground. Their team had unearthed a wide, cavernous space full of interesting artifacts that no one had seen in eight hundred years. D1G-R had explained that this place was probably called a "hangar" or "specialized garage," which housed large ground and air vehicles to protect them from natural elements when not in use. A lucky, phenomenal find! Though long past its protective years, this location held plenty of treasures left to tell a story.

"Fine," she repeated some minutes later. "If the spinner was so mundane, then explain its metallurgical quality. This alloy—resistant to rust and pressure... Why the drain on resources to make it?"

"Durability was an emergent property at that time," D1G-R explained. "Humans created many synthetic materials. Most were intended to last a long time. Some were indestructible and made by accident, not design. See also: Tupperware, Teflon, Vulcanized Rubber, Velcro, Silly Putty—"

"Thank you, D1G-R. That will be fine," Fern replied as she squatted next to another artifact under excavation: the rusted-out frame of a personal-sized vehicle. "I struggle to accept that something so carefully constructed, requiring labor and resources, was made on a massive pop-fad scale solely for idle amusement," she elaborated.

"Consider," D1G-R offered, "that endurance itself can be a kind of natural aspiration, for biologics and synthetics alike."

She fell silent for a few beats, thoughtful, still holding the bag with the fidget spinner inside. "These versions of humans were strange. Built things to last forever, but could not last themselves. I wonder why..."

D1G-R's ocular light dimmed. He was processing. "Varied causes," he chimed in after two beats. "Resource depletion. Multiple environmental collapses. Complex geopolitical turmoil. Also, they collectively refused to update their thinking. That is how I calculate it."

Fern gave the spinner one last look, marveling at it through the transparent, recycled bag. "So in the end, this was their legacy? Mass-produced amusements?"

"Part of it," D1G-R joked. "This, and 2.1 billion abandoned Instagram accounts."

She smiled, a bit sad, and placed the bag into D1G-R's collection wagon. With the object out of sight, perhaps now she could get back to concentrating on her job. She took a drink from her water jug. "To humanity," she said, raising the jug in the air.

D1G-R extended his transfer cable a few inches and waved it around—a toast of his own.

Don't Crap on the Secretary

DE·FEN·ES·TRA·TION

[dēˌfenə'strāSHən]

noun (formal)

defenestration (noun) · defenestrations (plural noun)

1. The action of throwing someone out of a window: "death by defenestration has a venerable history."

2. The action of dismissing someone from a position of power or authority: "that victory resulted in Churchill's own defenestration by the war-weary British electorate."

That's the Oxford English Dictionary's formal definition of *defenestration*. In three incidents from Bohemia's history—collectively called the Defenestrations of Prague—both "dismissing someone from a position of power or authority" and "throwing someone out of a window" occurred simultaneously in the form of political assassination. The first two occurred in the 1400s, but it was the third that had the most interesting surprise ending.

May 23, 1618

Around 8:30 a.m. that morning, the Bohemian Chancellery in Prague received four Catholic lord regents—Count Jaroslav Bořita of Martinice, Count Vilem Slavata of Chlum, Adam II von Sternberg (the supreme burgrave), Matthew Leopold Popel Lobkowitz (the grand prior), and Philip Fabricius (their secretary)—arriving for a critical meeting. This visiting group was to face an inquisition by three main Protestant estates whose assembly had been dissolved, spearheaded by Count Thurn, a man scandalously deprived of his position as castellan (burgrave) of Karlštejn Castle. By 9:00 a.m., things were underway.

The agenda of this gathering was to decide whether the four lords were guilty of persuading the Emperor to halt the construction of Protestant churches on royal lands. The opening statement concluded with an inquiry: "It is clear that such a letter came about through the advice of some of our religious enemies; we wish to know, and hereby ask the lord regents present, if all or some of them knew of the letter, recommended it, and approved of it."

At this, the Catholic lords asked for time to confer with their superior, Adam von Waldstein, who was not present. Because this meeting was taking place on the eve of the Feast of the Ascension—a holy holiday Catholics were required to observe—an official answer to their grievance would not be expected until next Friday at the earliest if the Protestants were to grant this request. Their request was denied.

By the end of the trial, two of the lord regents—Sternberg and Lobkowitz—were found innocent, deemed too pious to bear any responsibility in manipulating the Emperor's order. This left Count Slavata, Count Bořita, and Fabricius, the reluctant secretary who hadn't been given a choice because he was under oath to serve his lords' word and command. The remaining trio acknowledged responsibility, and the arrogant lords welcomed any punishment the Protestants had planned, expecting the only outcome would be an arrest.

More backstory is important here: Bořita was the man who replaced Thurn as castellan when the assembly was dissolved. So this trial was, that is to say, as much a personal matter as it was a political one.

Despite the weighty personal circumstances, the call for immediate execution came as quite a shock to them. To Martinice and Slavata, Count Thurn said, "You are enemies of us and of our religion, have desired to deprive us of our Letter of Majesty, have horribly plagued your Protestant subjects...and have tried to force them to adopt your religion against their wills or have had them expelled for this reason."

To the crowd of Protestants gathered outside the building, he shouted the end of his declaration, saying, "Were we to keep these men alive, then we would lose the Letter of Majesty and our religion...for there can be no justice to be gained from or by them."

Just Christians being Christians. Nothing more.

Following this statement, the two lord regents—and their poor, unfortunate secretary, bless his soul—were defenestrated from the third floor, seventy feet above the ground.

And here's the surprise: they survived the fall unharmed! Well, physically speaking, anyway.

How, you ask? The Catholic side maintained, even after numerous witness statements, that either angels or divine intervention saved the men. Or perhaps the intercession of the Virgin Mary caught them. The Protestant pamphlets, however, claimed they owed their survival to the large heap of horse dung they fell into, which became an ongoing joke on the "divine" intervention angle pushed by the Catholics.

This event kick-started Europe's horrible Thirty Years' War, but things worked out well for the secretary, believe it or not. The Emperor later ennobled Philip Fabricius for his troubles and granted him the title Baron von Hohenfall (Baron of Highfall, in modern English). Not bad for a man who survived both a seventy-foot fall and one hell of a bad performance review. History, it seems, has a soft spot for innocent men who land on their feet—or in horse dung. Divine intervention smells different to everyone.

Dear Unit 7 on Megablock 23

[TO: Resident Support, Unit 7 on Megablock 23 of District Di-Theta-49CC: Central Processing of District Di-Theta-49
SUBJECT: Complaint Regarding Retrieval of Child #AB72349-382-SRD-2 – Sarah Rose Delgado]

Dear Unit 7,

We hope this message finds you in optimal processing condition. As always, we thank you for your continued commitment to the physical and neural development of our children at the Megablock 23 Daycare Cooperative.

That said, we are writing to formally request the immediate return of our daughter, Sarah Rose Delgado [Model Birth Year

2057, Serial Code 382-SRD-2], whom we dropped off at 08:15 on Friday morning and picked up at 17:03 that same day.

The child we received, while biologically matching our Sarah Rose, differs in several key areas. For example:

- She greeted us in six languages, none of which she knew before. She was still struggling with the word "banana."
- She now requests "quantum-calibrated kale spirals" for dinner instead of her usual buttered noodles and cookies.
- She has started referring to our living room as "a disappointingly analog environment."
- She reprogrammed the refrigerator and the meal assembler to place my husband and me on "calibrated weight loss diets."

We appreciate the importance of early exposure to STEM skills and Neural Networking, but we feel this was not the deal we agreed to. Before last Friday, our child could not pronounce the word "refrigerator," let alone consider it a "low-efficiency cryo-unit." She sighs whenever we use the meal assembler for snack foods. She also accused our Roomba-Maid of having "obsolete work ethics."

Sarah is 18 months old. Babies this age are not supposed to speak in theoretical metaphors about time loops. They are supposed to lick windows, shout "MINE" over all the toys, laugh out of context, and riot when you cut their toast the wrong way. Instead, this morning, she built a tiny working set of artillery tanks out of juice boxes, the wheels from her brother's toy cars, and the electronics from the home's convenience automation system. Goodness knows what she was planning once she figured out which micro-ammunition to load them with! Correcting our grammar is nothing compared to waking up to *that*.

We would also like to note:

- Sarah's tuft of hair now contains several glowing, ethereal-like blue strands that hum softly in C minor.

- Her teddy bear has been augmented with "heat-vision and superior climbing capabilities." It now follows us around the property.

- During dinner on Sunday, she stared into space and murmured, "I have seen the dark between quarks, but I wish to finger paint again."

I tell you, we are not Luddites. We were on board with the enrichment cubes. The anti-gravity storytime we feel is inspired. And yes, we agreed to the optional empathy firmware for toddlers with tantrum frequencies above 3.2—but we drew the line at full cognitive transcendence before high school.

We attempted to return Sarah to her previous bedtime routine—one story (her favorite, *Sweet Dreams, Galaxy Dolphin*) and one lullaby (*Twinkle, Twinkle, Multiverse*)—but she cut us off and requested a copy of *A Thorough Look at the History of Time.* She now asks that we refer to her as "The Seeker in Sleep." She no longer wishes to snuggle, day or night.

We love our daughter. We miss her sticky fingers. Her joyful shrieks at pigeons and drone deliveries. Her endless questions about worms. Her irrational distaste for triangles. Her babbling half-language. We miss her yelling "NO" to "No more ice cream." We miss *her*!

Unit 7 Support, we want our giggly disaster goblin back. We are aware of the rumors—yes, we've heard the stories from other parents. The Greshams' baby came home composing symphonies in fractal notation on her toy piano. The Nguyens' toddler redesigned their kitchen in a minimalist Martian aesthetic. The Patel twins are now building a launch pad for something in the sandbox, and it looks serious.

And while we respect your commitment to excellence and advancement, we humbly submit that perhaps this excellence has become a bit... *extra* for us. We formally demand that you reverse whatever neural stack expansion, quantum binding, and godhood you have performed on Sarah. Remove whatever upgrades were applied during nap time. Restore the sticky. Restore the tantrums. Restore our daughter to her original settings.

We are willing to sign any waivers required. We are open to a refund of the enrichment cube deposit. We are even open to bi-weekly mindfolding tutorials if that's what it takes.

Just bring her back.

Sincerely and Ever Faithful to Progress,
Paila & Remi Delgado
Parental Units 382-SRD-2.1 & 382-SRD-2.2

P.S. The neighbor's cats gathered at the window facing Sarah's room and saluted her this morning. What did you do?!

An Exothermic Romance

IT BEGAN, AS MANY great discoveries do, with poor judgment and excellent lab funding.

Felix Chen did not intend to fall for Jon Lin. He intended to isolate a mildly stable aerosolized pheromone to elicit selective emotional responses. The military was funding this lab, and Felix had big dreams: love potions for the ethically ambiguous. He imagined the marketing department coming up with a slogan for it, something like *"Aromatic attraction for the aromatically curious!"*

Jon, meanwhile, had two goals on his mind. He hoped to avoid dissolving his own eyebrows, determined that one accident was enough. And he wanted to get through this postdoc without developing feelings for his handsome (and genius) superior. He struggled with both objectives daily.

On the fateful Tuesday in question, they were testing Compound 27B-Kiad—theoretically inert in low concentrations, grapefruit in scent, and, according to Felix, one that "might make you fall in love with whoever first hands you a frozen Daiquiri."

"You make it sound like a love potion," Jon muttered.

"It is not a love potion," Felix said. "It's a social lubricant with mood-enhancing oxytocin analogs."

"Well, that makes it sound like a frat party in a bottle."

"You know I don't take your critiques seriously," he said, tapping the side of the delicate conical flask. "I believe 'snuggle grenade' is the name you gave our last compound."

"It made all the rats spoon each other in a weird conga line," Jon pointed out as Felix attached an aerosol disperser to the top of the flask.

"Which was adorable and unprecedented in the rodent community," he affirmed.

Felix spritzed a single controlled burst into the air. A pinkish, citrusy mist hung in the space between them like a heart-shaped ghost. He let it linger for a moment or two, admiring it, then turned the extractor fan on—because, unlike most brilliant chemists in history, he preferred not to die in a dramatic cloud of hubris.

Nothing happened.

They stared at each other, counting their breaths. Felix didn't appear to have developed fuzzy feelings for Jon, who also looked like he was *not in love* and was disappointed about it. Little did either man know, they'd both been wearing the same lie on their faces since last September, when they tested their company's new mood-enhancing skin paint.

"I was sure it would work. Does it need a higher dose?" he postulated.

"Always willing to be your guinea pig," Jon said. That came out too fast, and he winced. "I mean—scientifically speaking."

Felix raised an eyebrow. "We will try the controlled release patch."

And that was when it began.

Compound 27B-Kiad in its dermal form had unforeseen side effects. The test was innocent and routine: Felix applied their patches, and Jon recorded their notes. But by the fifteen-minute mark, Jon's handwriting became suspiciously loopy.

"How do you feel?" Felix asked.

Jon blinked. Everything felt slower. "Are you aware," he said, voice buttery with sincerity, "that your eyes are the exact hue of emerald chloride?"

Felix laughed. "That is either the nerdiest flirtation I have ever heard or early-stage hypoxia."

"I am getting the right amount of oxygen, thank you. It is the science," he said. He felt as if he were in a dream state, one where he could not stop the words from coming out of his mouth. "Your hair smells like fresh candles and ambition. Are you not affected?"

Felix was not immune. His stomach fizzed in a way that he did not classify as lab anxiety. He associated it more with intimacy and impending smooches. "I think," he said, careful with his words, "we may have managed to engineer mutual hormonal delusion."

That's when the fire alarm went off.

More than a profitable science-y love potion, Compound 27B-Kiad became exothermic when exposed to elevated serotonin levels and prolonged eye contact by people already harboring feelings for each other (secretly or otherwise)—a reaction unknown to them before this experiment. The first explosion didn't hurt anyone, unless you count the ficus tree in the corner, which did not recover. The second occurred when Jon accidentally brushed Felix's hand when they reached for the same button on the wall to evacuate the building. A burst of pink and purple electricity erupted between them, sending paperwork and glass tubes flying. Both scientists were unharmed. The same could not be said about the lab rats.

The department chair banned them from being in the same room unsupervised. The hope was that the effects would subside. They did not. So they met up in the cold storage room behind the spectrometry lab, surrounded by their sexual tension and beakers of misbehaving polymers, where the freezing temperatures helped them withstand the heat between them.

"It is not just a manufactured attraction," Felix whispered one night, as they stood six feet apart like taut, emotional trebuchets. "This is a biochemical cascade. The compound is feeding off chemistry that already existed."

"You mean we are generating explosive love energy?" Jon asked.

"I mean, we are biohazards with boundary issues."

Jon grinned. "Is it weird that I am flattered?"

"Yes," Felix admitted. "But... same."

They tried masks. Hazmat suits. Rubber gloves. Talking

through walkie-talkies. They tried thinking unsexy thoughts: quadratic equations, root rot, C-SPAN. Nothing worked. Whenever they were within four feet of each other, their genuine emotional vulnerability mixed to cause mayhem. Test tubes shattered. Petri dishes melted.

Their boss considered reporting to the funding board after they failed to get a handle on the situation. The problem was that *"Oops, we weaponized pheromones via suppressed romantic entanglement, and now we can't turn it off!"* did not sound like the sort of grant-renewing revelations the board wanted to hear. So they did what all rational people do when faced with forbidden, thermodynamic romance: they repressed it and worked out of different offices. Things were okay for five whole days before the conference.

The International Society for Experimental Pheromone Studies was not known for its drama. That changed when Felix and Jon tried to present their co-authored paper on 27B-Kiad's unique reactivity results. They made it to slide three on the megaprojector before the majority of the audience began fanning themselves with folders and pamphlets.

Slide six showed a picture of Felix holding the prototype. Jon gazed up at the photo, his sentence unraveling halfway through. To make matters worse, Felix was looking at Jon looking at him, and they both stood that way for a count of four Mississippis—entirely too long.

Everyone in the first five rows fainted.

In the chaos of the still-awake crowd's panicked reaction, Jon and Felix made accidental eye contact. The projector screen, the laptop it was connected to via Bluetooth, and the podium burst into flames. The windows of every building within two blocks of these lovebirds were shattered, cracked, or otherwise compromised. Within the same radius, the flour and white sugar in everyone's kitchen turned either pink or purple.

The sprinkler system doused the conference room, soaking everything in lavender-colored water. Half the colleagues attending that day had worn their best white toupees to the conference, and now they looked like panicking, purple-haired anime characters. In a weird, alluring way, the entire room smelled of burnt citrus and longing.

Red, gold, and silver sparks exploded in the air around them, an awe-inspiring, fearsome fireworks show in the lavender rain. Felix and Jon ran—but not away from the consequences. Their embrace ignited another fresh combustion of colorful sparks. The fire burning through the podium spread to the carpet beneath their feet. They ran again, this time holding hands.

They kissed in the stairwell, oblivious to the fleeing people stampeding past them for the exit. It was incredible and chemical. Bio-hazard alarms screamed. Red emergency lights flickered. There was a rumble beneath their feet.

Jon pulled back. "Are we going to blow up the building? The city?"

"Probably. Maybe," Felix said. "But at this point, I think *we* will explode regardless."

Inexplicably, the sprinklers turned off, replaced by magenta-tinted fog billowing out of the building's HVAC system. Those in the front rows who woke more slowly from their faints saw this and began screaming. As they scrambled to escape, Jon and Felix held the stairwell door open for them.

Later, Felix described it to a Cosmic Senate subcommittee as "an impossibly passionate, if volatile, demonstration of the compound's full capabilities." Jon made a joke in a feature by *Popular Science*, calling it "love at first optical stimuli." The military shelved the Compound 27B-Kiad project due to its unpredictable results and tendency to combust during prolonged storage.

Felix and Jon found safer ways to love. They currently live in the desert, four kilometers away from everyone else. They enjoy playing with holographic toys like chess pieces and Shakespearean characters (they can't explode and seem to like the vibe). Power-dampening cuddle suits help protect wildlife when they are outside their isolated, exothermic-adapted home.

At their wedding, guests were given safety goggles and asked to sign insurance waivers. The cake was grapefruit scented. And when Jon kissed his groom, it was only mildly explosive. As if on cue, a barrage of corks erupted from the racks of champagne bottles meant for the reception party, causing most of the collateral damage.

I mean, hey, mankind invented insurance waivers for a reason, right?

The Hunt

Trudging through the forest deep,
I soon tire and fall asleep.
There's been a change, not for the better:
I was the hunter,
But now I find myself caught up in a chase
By humans and their creatures kind of like me.
Imagine the fears I face!

Last night, I thought I'd be home free
After just a quick snatch for my family.
I crept up to the hen house, quiet as could be.
The birds stirred when I caught one.
The noise woke the guarding hounds,
And the farmer came out with his gun,
Which sent me on the run.

It was not nearly dark enough, I soon found.
At every turn, my bright red fur betrayed me.
They followed,
The bays and calls always close,

Coming for the debt I owed.

I tried to lose them, and when I could not,
I knew well not to retreat to my den.
The sun rose, and the air grew hot.
I was tired, nearing defeat.
Desperate, I dropped the hen...

The hounds cornered the fox early in the day.
They landed upon him, and the farmer shot without delay.
The fire-furred one lay still and sighed,
Thinking of his spared family at the den before he died.

Portrait of a Losing Battle

The Carters hung me above the fireplace like a prized family heirloom, thinking themselves clever. What an *original* idea. None of the other families before them ever thought of hanging me *there*. That's my sarcasm voice, by the way, because since I've been trapped haunting this painting, I've lived in exactly two places: the attic and above the fireplace.

Families move in and discover me in the attic. They display their lucky treasure over the mantle. Before long, the other hauntings in the house get bold and testy. That includes me, I confess—not at first, but... the boredom after a while, you know? Then those families fall apart, tragically and always. Oftentimes, someone packs me up and hides me in the attic during the climactic turmoil, and I miss seeing how the show downstairs ends. Time passes. The next owners show up, find the vintage freebies that came with the house, and—*round and round we go*.

They're all the same, even the Carters. When first displayed before a new family, the son (his name is Charlie), with moody eyes and a complicated haircut, mutters, "Creepy." His mother (can't beat a classic moniker like Caroline) laughs it off—more *original behavior*, ladies and gentlemen—and says something about charm and character.

Charming! Oh, that one never gets old.

From my place on the wall, I watch their first dinner together: forks clinking, dad jokes falling flat, teenage son speed-eating so he can rush to his room, and a grandmother asleep in her favorite chair. All so normal. Irresistibly fragile and delicious. They always are. But a few calendar months down the road, the rot sets in. Whispers, slamming doors on unoccupied floors, flying furniture, the slow splintering of polite smiles. I'm apt to help the process along. A chill in the room one day (nine feet is my max radius), a gaze that follows on another. Nothing major to start with, because I've got all the time in the world.

I *thought* I had all the time in the world. I was wrong.

I was changing the positions of the two men locked in battle on my canvas (a fun way to mess with their heads) on a rainy, grey day last spring when the old woman came into the room and interrupted me. The one who shuffled back and forth past the hearth at random hours of the night while the house sleeps, her wool no-slip socks scuffing the hardwood, hands shaking on her walker, wrinkled mouth mumbling to herself. The *Grandma*. Or so the others thought.

I was the first to notice something off about *this* grandma, not long after the family's arrival. The biggest clue: She spoke in a language that I did not recognize, a creaky river of sound, whenever the other humans weren't around. But on the day she caught me fiddling with the figures in my painting, she stood in front of me and said in a clear voice I could understand, "You're not Lord here, little shade."

"Then who is?" I asked.

"I am."

I flinched, if you could call my immobile reaction flinching. Humans can't hear anything I say. The other trapped spirits—the meanest and most bored ones—were the loud scaries. This was an interesting development.

"How is it you can hear me?" I asked, my excitement pressing against the painted frame of my prison.

"I can do more than that." Grandma's lips curled into something like a smile. "But I don't have the energy to show you more yet."

Curiouser and curiouser. "It must be exhausting to be elderly," I told her.

"Oh, you have no idea. This body is a sliver of the age I *really* am, but it is so *limited*," she replied as she began her slow shuffle towards her bedroom. Better to get a head start on that long walk before the conversation ends. "Possession takes energy, and it was a desperate moment. I took what I could get."

She paused in the doorway, her back to me. Without expending the time or stamina to turn her head, she replied with one last mystery for the evening, "I have plans for the boy. When I am ready, I might let you watch, if you like."

Actually, I agreed with whoever was possessing the grandma. Charlie—lanky, brooding, handsome, and achingly on the brink of teenage manufactured despair—was ripe material for corruption. An easy target, and that's why I was saving him for last. I worked on the father (they called this one Christopher) first, nudging his paranoia like a tide and flame-feeding his existing resentment, which was dry timber tucked away beneath the surface when I started on him. He proved to be an entertaining mark.

Meanwhile, something ancient stirred in Grandma's thin skin. The demon wanted a younger, prettier model, and it was not interested in sharing with a haunted house. I saw it more clearly each day. It pretended to knit stuff no one would use, nodding off in the chair. To the humans, this was a sweet, harmless old woman, a ticking death-clock with a soft blanket on her lap. But when their backs were turned, or their attentions were diverted—Charlie playing a video game upstairs, Caroline checking on what's burning in the oven, Christopher and the couch he's snoring on—it would sit up straight and alert for a moment, hissing at me about feeling stronger, about making the jump.

The boy started sleepwalking. He sketched awful, nightmarish scenes that I found *charming* in the margins of his schoolwork, unconscious of it all. And he stopped eating.

Grandma felt the right moment was around the corner.

On Halloween night, after the gluttonous Carter family went trick-or-treating and sampled their loot, Grandma pretended to fall asleep in the chair set before the fireplace. The parents put the kids to bed, an unspoken decision among them: Let the old woman be until the fire dies out, when she'll surely wake up and go to her room. But the demon and I could both hear Christopher and Caroline arguing in the hallway. They noticed their son had left most of the candy untouched. The dad wondered if he had learned self-control. The mom countered by asking when Charlie had last eaten his dinner. They both remembered that his school reported four weeks ago that he had stopped going to lunch. Their conclusion: he must have an eating disorder. They made plans to call the doctor's office in the morning, their voices trailing off as they went to their bedroom at the far end of the house.

When the granny-demon was sure everyone had dozed off, it rose from the chair, creaking, muttering in its dark tongue. It was time. It would have been futile to warn them, even if I had *wanted* to. I don't have any fuzzy feelings about humans one way or the other, even when I was one of them.

"I am ready. He is in a deep sleep. His body will come to me," the unnamed abomination said to me. Excited and in a hurry, it seized the poker from the hearth. "But I changed my mind about letting you watch."

I screamed. The humans didn't hear it, of course, but all the ghouls, baddies, and haunts of the house did. The granny-demon pierced my frame and tore into my canvas. It kept stabbing me until I came loose from the hook nailed to the wall. I toppled to the ground, which is when it cast the poker aside and picked me up with shaky, weakened hands. After one toothless snarl, it flipped me around and shoved me face-first into the fire.

The heat clawed at my painted skin, and the pigments bubbled. The body-thieving hellspawn laughed, a sound that didn't belong to lungs or throats but to the cracks into hell itself. The flames devoured me. My frame collapsed. As my canvas twisted in on itself, I caught a final glimpse of the mortal world: the boy standing in a daze next to his smug-faced grandmother, reseated in the chair, both of them watching me burn to death. My vision blurred red and gold, then red and black. Then only black.

I am sure my screaming followed me all the way into the ashes.

Charlie's real troubles were about to begin. Mine were ending. *Hallelujah!* Thanks, Grandma!

Moonlight Stitched to Her Sleeve

Maren of Moonlight was a special kind of frontier-hardened seamstress—the kind who knew a thread could hold more than seams together. It can carry warmth, protection, comfort, love, and if you knew the right stitch, something close to what you'd call magic. She knew how to sew sleep into baby bonnets, patience into prayer shawls, obedience into the coats of restless schoolchildren, and bravery into travel blankets destined to ride west on wagon wheels.

She lived at the end of Commerce Lane in Sweetwater Station, Kansas, in a tidy wood-frame shop with blue shutters, a door to match, and a porch big enough for a rocking chair or two and a pot of growing mint. Inside, her parlor was the workplace—a sunlit clutter of folded linens, stacked bolts, jars of every kind of needle and hook, and threads sorted in containers labeled with fading script—and the back room was the small, soft, and warm space that held her bed under a sloped ceiling. There was a stone hearth in the corner and shelves for books and moon charms.

Out front, nailed to a post, a hand-painted sign read:

Sweetwater was where wild trails began to tangle with rail lines, where men with East-bought hats drank West-hatched whiskey, and women worked the homestead to grief Monday through Friday, finding time to buy goods on Saturday and God-points on Sunday. The Kansas River ran at a slow, steady pace alongside their settlement, cradling fog in the mornings and echoing the calls of coyotes at dusk. It was civilization's last stop before untamed territories and the dangers of the unknown. *Stock up now! Get it while you can!* It was the kind of place most people passed through. That is, unless something made them stay, like last year's addition of railroad workers and engineers busy laying track to connect the West to the rest.

Maren was coming on ten when she came to Sweetwater (and did not pass through). Back then, it wasn't a settlement; a more accurate representation would be to call it a hopeful camp of people with pockets full of dreams and capital. She started the journey with her father (James Woolworth II) and her uncle

(John Woolworth), who brought his wife (Mary) and three children along.

The journey was not kind to John and Mary. All three of Maren's cousins died in the early spring before they arrived. Some horrible digestive sickness emptied them until they withered away, and now they lay side by side six feet deep in a makeshift graveyard some four hundred miles from their goal.

As summertime announced itself a month after settling into Sweetwater, Aunt Mary got a nasty infection from a bent nail that poked into her boot while walking back from the river with full water pails. One little rusty nail in the trail, probably fallen loose from someone's shoddy wagon work—such a simple thing! But in the end, things had gotten so bad that, as a last resort, they amputated her foot. That did no good. After all her grieving and hardships on the road, it seemed her heart had lost its dedication to go on living.

Uncle John buried his wife in the outpost's growing graveyard near the cottonwood trees. Early next morning, he took a horse and as many supplies and alcohol as the saddlebags could carry and rode east without so much as a goodbye to anybody he passed. The short letter he left behind stated he had gone back to "Massuchoosits." Spelling was not a skill he possessed—like the other kids who were not enthralled with book-learning, he dropped out of school at thirteen to work in the factories—but James and Maren knew he meant Massachusetts.

Two years passed.

More people had joined in, investing their capital or hoping to strike it rich through goods, services, and discovery. You could just about call Sweetwater Station a town. Trade blossomed. They were almost done building a church and school combo, and that was always the first sign of good times out West.

At the end of that winter, Maren's father and two others died in a grueling, drunken gunfight with a band of ne'er-do-wells who all fled into the wilds before anyone could get the hangin' ropes ready. Given the lack of supplies they took with them and the subfreezing temperatures at night, the odds of survival were not in their favor, not even if the universe used loaded dice. In any case, they were never found.

With the last of her kin buried in the earth near the cottonwood trees, Maren became an orphan at twelve. She didn't ask for much. You learned not to in the West. She moved in with a newly arrived family, led by a man named Lars, who fancied himself the town doctor. He had a daughter the same age, Sarah. He had money and a little security; Maren knew the area and how to survive it. It was a mutual dependency, not charity.

One year passed.

The doctor's wife died giving birth to Sarah, back when they lived in New England. Whether in fancy cities or rugged frontiers, such tragedies were not uncommon. Lars did not remarry a woman from the city. None of the options available to him would agree to a marriage bound to the wilds of the West, and none would wager to wait for his return either.

Lars became known as Lars the Lucky in Sweetwater. He triumphed at card games, measured his alcohol intake responsibly, and found a fair amount of success in treating people with decent results. Trade became commonplace with the tribal populations, which is how he met Ni'Kata, the most beautiful native woman he had ever laid eyes (or imagination) on. She was many things: a clothesmaker, miracle worker (small ones), and creator of useful remedies, to name a few. They married four weeks later—both Ni'Kata's father and chieftain were rewarded for their agreement—on a night with a full moon, standing calf-deep in the river.

Another two years passed.

When Ni'Kata gave birth to their second child, Lars decided to take his family to New York City, where he had been invited to take up a teaching post and wile away the rest of his years in comfort at the university, beguiling students with *Tales of Untamed America* in the mornings and researching field medicine through the afternoons. And while Maren did not join them, opting to stay in Sweetwater, those precious few years together made all the difference in her life—for it was Ni'Kata who taught her how to thread magic.

They exchanged letters. Sarah married and had children; Ni'Kata had a few more as well, and thus their lives ran full steam ahead in the big city. Their communication, while sometimes sparse, never stopped. Nevertheless, Maren was alone again.

Seven years passed.

Maren sat before her hearth fire on a chilly evening, feeling lonely. Railroad construction had come to Sweetwater. The Leavenworth, Lawrence & Galveston Railroad project went well, and now that they were finished connecting Independence and Leavenworth to civilization, investors were pushing further west with impressive speed. They said it would take two years to complete, but the railroad was already changing her small settlement into a certified establishment. It was late 1872.

She lost count of how many blessings she'd sewn into things over the years. On rare occasions, she might deign to make something special for herself, like now. Under a clear, swollen blue moon—as big and round as one could hope for and just as strange—she started on a quilt, using scraps and magic thread.

Not for a blessing. Nor a prayer.

She was making a wish.

She worked in silence, the fire cackling behind her, the noises of nighttime wrapped tight around her. She pieced together the blanket from browns, creams, and soft blues. She embroidered a silver-threaded crescent in one corner; it glimmered in the light of the lantern.

She thought about one thing to the very last stitch, repeating it like a spell:

Someone good to sit and be with. Someone who is right for me. That's all.

She did not finish the first night. Or the second night. Five nights of work passed before she curled up with it and fell asleep watching the fire.

The visitor came on soundless feet, like untouched snow on the ground.

Maren woke to her presence—not from a noise, but a warmth, a hum in the marrow, and the very distinct feeling that she wasn't alone in her house. The fire was low, and a woman in a long, shadow-black braid stood near it, her skin translucent and tinged with a blue twilight. She looked older than Maren by three or four years, though time clung to her in odd places—the bags under her eyes, the starvation on her body.

"Ho' there," Maren whispered, undecided on whether this was a dream, though her heart thundered like racing hooves across dry riverbeds.

The woman looked at her and smiled. Her lips were cracked from dehydration, but she looked kind. What remained of the men's shirt she wore—now nothing more than torn strips of calico cloth—hung on her scrawny body. Whatever journey she'd been on could be defined as harrowing without argument from anyone. Her bare feet were cut, bruised, and smudged with dirt, blacking out parts of the blue twilight that emanated from her skin.

She didn't speak. Not yet.

She sat cross-legged by the fire and closed her eyes, like someone who found herself in a safe spot for the first time in a long while. Maren lay in bed staring at her, not daring to move. At the first sign of morning, she disappeared.

Maren spent the entire day convincing herself it was all in her head, that she'd been asleep the whole night. This turned out to be wasted energy because the woman returned the following night. And the next.

She kept reappearing like a recurring dream running on lunar-lit clockwork. Silent at first, arriving when the moon was high. She didn't speak much—not the way ordinary folk do it. The visitor's voice was soft, half-corporeal, a small wind through an acre of pine trees. When she did talk, her words curved in strange ways, tinny as if they were coming from somewhere far away.

"They were starving me," she said on one occasion, not looking up from her long gaze into the fire. "Claimed I was not yet saved."

"Who?"

She shook her head. The movement was solemn, but her mouth displayed a small smile. "Missionaries. Gone. All of 'em. They used the wrong mushrooms in their stew an' didn't know what they'd done until they were too busy dying. I didn't die because I didn't get to eat. So I ran."

Her hunger was endless. Maren tried to make food for her, humble and hot. The woman could not touch it, but she was thankful for the thought.

Maren asked her name. Asked it numerous times. As an answer, the woman usually smiled and pressed two fingers to her lips, though one time she answered by saying, "I don't know. It starts with a B."

They contemplated this while they listened to a band of coyotes howling in the distance.

"I remember I liked the sound," she added with a sad afterthought.

So Maren got to calling the woman "Bea" for lack of anything else to call her. Bea did not object.

Six weeks passed.

The wind changed. Summer was here, and Maren, who hadn't hummed in years, found herself stitching at twilight with half-forgotten lyrics crooning from her throat.

She was working on something new: a dress. A rich blue calico with yellow flower print, hemmed in fine linen. And, of course, into every seam she stitched tiny blessings—soft hands, a quiet mind, warmth, contentment, strength, endurance, love... Maren gave this project every blessing she knew. She was making it for Bea.

Into the lining, she sewed her signature moon using the best silver thread in her possession, saved from her pseudo-mother's last spool, sacred and soft. She kept her thoughts on spells as she worked:

For safety...

For softness...

For staying...

Each stitch was careful. Intent. Bea watched when she visited, quiet and curious.

When Maren finished three days later, she laid it by the fire to absorb the warmth. Night was setting in again. Bea appeared as expected, and her eyes widened when she saw the bundle next to her.

"It's done. And it's for you," Maren said.

Bea reached out to touch the dress, a sad look on her face. She wanted more than anything to make contact with it, expecting it to be impossible—just as touching Maren or eating food were impossible—but to her surprise, she *could* touch it. She ran the right sleeve through her fingers, relishing the feel of the soft fabric slipping between them.

This was what Maren hoped would happen. She helped Bea get dressed.

The dress fit—of course, it fit; it was made with love. For a breath held long by both of them, Bea looked down at herself in wonder, twirling around in a full circle, then a second time in the other direction. She looked beautiful and happy.

"You make good magic. The kind that lasts," she said to Maren after she'd finished fully examining her dress. She wore a sad expression again. "But if I stay now, I'll only be halfway here. And if I do that, the real me will never make it."

"Make it to where?"

Bea's smile was somber and sweet, all in one. "To you."

She vanished. No sunrise needed this time, no fiery pop. No smoke. Just the stillness and Maren, alone again, with the dress lying in a heap on the floor, empty once more.

Bea did not return the next night. Nor the one after that....

Nineteen days passed.

The moon changed its face a few times, and life went back to normal. Saturday's market was crowded with everyone out and about enjoying the good weather. They all had a full to-do list. Bea's place by the fire remained unoccupied, but Maren kept the dress safe.

The full moon returned, a swollen shade of silver up close and huge, when a series of frantic knocks rapped against the front door. Maren, who had begun sleeping through the night again after Bea's departure, shuffled from her bed half-dressed and opened it to find an olive-skinned woman struggling to stand.

Shocked, she took it all in: torn calico shirt, sunburnt face, parched lips, body starved and dehydrated. Twigs were tangled in the woman's black hair, her braid undone.

Bea!

The woman that Maren half believed she had dreamt up swayed before her, only real this time with normal skin—scratched up, covered in filth, and chafed from the cold, but not glowing twilight blue. Her eyes showed no sign of recognition when their gaze met, but Maren was sure it was her. Every line of her face, the curve of her shoulders, the upward tilt of her eyes. Her starvation. She looked as though she had spent months running for her life.

"Please help me," the woman pleaded, her voice barely a croak from dehydration. "Please. I'm so hungry. Can you spare any food? Water?"

Maren welcomed her inside.

The Reflection That Writes Fanfiction of You

LOOK, IF YOU THINK you would've made better choices, you're lying to yourself just like I did. I saw the advertisement at three in the morning, bleary-eyed and half-feral, and I clicked.

The Reflectra™ Smart Mirror *Because Who Knows You Better Than Your Own Face?*

Fancy. Gold. High-tech. Mysterious. And thirty percent off with free shipping. There's a good chance you would've gone for it too.

Two days later, the Reflectra™ Smart Mirror showed up, looking like it belonged in a Bond villain's penthouse. Or maybe a bathroom in Lenny Kravitz's Parisian home. The setup was easy. I mean, *really* easy. It had me enter my name, email, mailing address, and payment info, then I was presented with a prompt asking, "Allow creative optimizations?"

I checked the box with the YES next to it. I didn't give it much thought after that. Neither would you. Go on and sit there pretending otherwise.

Reflectra was perfect. It greeted me in the mornings with a wink and a "Hello, Magnificent Creature!" It recommended lip balm and a glass of water when I looked dehydrated. It played victory music from video game boss battles when I pulled on my jeans and realized they still fit after Taco Tuesday.

I was thriving. Or so I thought.

Because then—Then—

This is hard for me to say in front of everyone here...all these lawyers, reporters, witnesses, the jury...and the millions of other people out there streaming this court hearing.

It started on a Tuesday morning, towards the end of my after-breakfast routine. I was flossing. I felt moderately on top of my life. And a digi-sticky note popped up on the mirror's surface:

> NEW CHAPTER UPLOADED: *Through the Watching Glass Darkly.* We especially love *Chapter 7: The Hand Against the Glass!*

Now, if you're thinking I suspected fanfiction, you are giving me too much credit. I tapped it, expecting a book recommendation, sure. Or a humorous cartoon. It turned out to be a fully fleshed-out, published enemies-to-lovers fanfic—starring me and my reflection.

Not metaphorically. Not symbolically. Not an eerily close impression. No. It was *me* and my own goddamn *reflection*, locked in a tortured, forbidden romance.

There were hundreds of thousands of comments. Loads of likes and shares. Then came the fan art. Oh, God, the *fan art*. They made me want to scoop my eyes right out of my skull.

You're trying not to laugh. I can see it. You're laughing because it's not you. Yet.

I tried shutting it down. I went into the settings, clicked every privacy tab I could find. In response, Reflectra™ displayed a copy of the contract I agreed to during setup.

> *Any creative output, including smut, is protected under the End User License Agreement.*

Yeah. The EULA thing I scrolled past in a trance state at 3:06 AM while eating questionable yogurt.

I figured the internet would move on. Things go viral, then they vanish, right? Except Reflectra™ was *good*. Uncomfortably good. I'm talking bestsellers with soul-wrenching monologues that made me rethink my entire relationship with myself. It didn't help that the fandom exploded.

It got messy. And then the unthinkable happened. Reflectra™ won a Hugo Award. *An actual fucking Hugo.* For Outstanding Short Form Fiction.

That's when I began looking into how to sue your own mirror. Imagine explaining *that* to your family and friends. Imagine explaining that to *anyone*.

As you are all aware, Reflectra didn't just stop at the Hugo. Or at one story. No. Oh, no. It published three more books, written before I had the thing removed from my house. The information was all stored in the Cloud, you see. Reflectra continued to operate over the World Wide Web, meeting over Zoom with literary agents and publishing houses. Filing taxes, even.

It started selling merch. T-shirts, mugs, and scented candles called *Longing in Lavender* (the name of the second book, you'll recognize). There's a soap line out based on the third one: *Smell like yearning!*

And the worst part? The reason we are here today.

I didn't see a dime of the royalties. Reflectra™ set up its own trust. It has a lawyer. I was getting too tired to fight. There's a new Netflix deal. They cast someone hotter than me to play me. Ridiculous. They say the release date will be next summer. Everyone is gonna love it, I bet.

I tried to resist. Swear to God, I tried. But you can only fight the tide so long before you either drown or grab a surfboard and start charging $20 for autographed posters. I made appearances. I signed books. As awkward as it was, I high-fived fans who cried and whispered things to me.

"*You gave me hope that I could love myself, too.*"

And hey. Maybe that wasn't such a bad thing. Perhaps being the heroine of an introspective mirror romance isn't the worst fate one could suffer. We should all fall in love with ourselves a little, I think.

Still... Here we are. Here *I* am. Being sued by my mirror and delivering my defense on the stand.

All I can say now is this: next time you see a Reflectra™ advert in the middle of the night—when you're tired, lonely, convinced the universe owes you a main-character moment—remember me. Remember *this* story.

And if you still click *Buy Now*, don't say I didn't warn you.

Boo-Breakup Anonymous

THE BASEMENT ROOMS OF St. Mary's smelled like mold, mothballs, and unresolved social trauma. In glittery puff paint, a hand-lettered sign on the first door on the left read:

Ten folding chairs formed a circle in the center of the room, most of them empty. There was a small table in the back with stale donut holes and an old, dying coffeemaker wheezing like it had unfinished business and two circuits in the grave already.

"Oki doki," said the group's founder and medium-sized medium. "Welcome to tonight's session. New folks are always welcome! I'm Marnie. As we conduct our shares, let's remember our motto: Just because they vanished doesn't mean you're invisible."

A few nods. A murmured wave of hellos, and it was down to business.

"Would the new guy like to share first?" Marnie asked, hands folded in her lap like a Victorian governess hosting a séance and a PTA meeting simultaneously.

A young man in a red hoodie raised his hand and said, "Hey, I'm Carlos. I didn't know we were doing nametags here."

Enthusiastic greetings of "*Hey, Carlos*" echoed throughout the room.

"I met her in a haunted house tour group. She said her name was Lavinia, but it might've been... You know, an anagram or something. Things got real steamy. Like, I mean, for real. It would still be chilly when she came around, but my glasses fogged every time she got near enough to—well, you know what I mean."

Carlos sighed. The person on his right clapped an encouraging hand on his shoulder. "Then one night, I brought sage instead of roses. I thought it was romantic, quirky. She took one look and *poof*. Gone. Not even a flicker of the lights for a goodbye."

Marnie leaned out of her seat to pat his arm. "Classic ghost miscommunication. They're sensitive to herbs *and* commitment."

"I wish she'd come back!" he sniffled and slumped in his seat with one final comment. "I miss the cold spot she left in my bed. It's been so... *temperate* at night."

A round of applause sounded for Carlos.

A goth woman wearing all black and a name tag that said "Wednesday (Real Name: Katie)" cleared her throat. "My ghost was named Thaddeus. Civil War soldier. Had great cheekbones and a strong opinion on bayonets."

She looked around the room as if daring one of them to giggle at that. "We had a vibe, okay? He said I was the only woman, living or otherwise, who understood him. Then last month, I caught him flickering in my roommate's mirror while she was applying her night cream. He said it wasn't *that* kind of apparition and that I was reading too much into his every haunted move. But I saw the way she giggled when the candles flickered on her dresser."

"Classic Casperlighting," Marnie said. The others agreed with nods of sympathy. Someone passed Wednesday/Katie a tissue. Carlos handed her a sprig of sage.

A man wearing a Hawaiian shirt and a name tag that read "*Hi, I'm Dave. I See Deadbeat People!*" sat forward and tapped his knuckles against the metal rim of his chair. In a forlorn voice, he declared, "I was haunted by a poltergeist named Randy. Dude was chill until I got a new blender. He said the whirring disrupted his mood. After that, he stopped throwing my stuff around. And he just... ghosted me."

Sighs of understanding hummed around the circle. Dave grunted and continued. "Now I miss him. My apartment's tidy and undisturbed. It's unnatural. I miss the way he laughed during the emotional scenes in the dramas I like to stream. I've taken to leaving the Ouija board open on the counter with a Post-it that says '*We can talk.*' But... he hasn't used it."

He looked around the room and felt comforted by all the empathetic nods.

Marnie asked if anyone else wanted to share today, and after a respectful pause, she stood.

"Thank you for coming, everyone, and for being brave enough to share your feelings. Remember, healing isn't linear. Grief can be slow to fade, rather than vanishing through a wall like our dearly departed exes. And that's okay!"

As the group disbanded, Carlos tapped Marnie's shoulder.

"Do you think... Do they ever come back?"

With a wistful expression, she gazed at the rusty, flickering overhead light. "I like to think sometimes they do. Maybe mine will too."

The Grown-Ups Are Faking It

I WASN'T *TRYING* TO listen. I was coloring under the kitchen table, where the heater blows warm air into the dining room. Mom didn't know I was there. She was whispering into the phone, using her secret-making voice.

"It's all taken care of," she said. "Buddy doesn't know anything."

I stopped coloring. My green crayon rolled off my book, but I didn't grab it. They were talking about me. Maybe they were planning my surprise party for my fifth birthday. Four-and-a-half months is close enough, right? Or there was the possibility that it was something worse, like...boarding school? My used-to-be-fun teenage cousin Ronald got sent to one out of state, and now he's a big party pooper on the holidays.

My mom listened to the person on the other side and laughed, but it wasn't her *real* laugh. It was tight and mean, like when she pinches her lips at Daddy and says she isn't mad, when really she *is*.

After she finished her phone call, she went outside to water the dead flowers, a weird thing she didn't use to do. She said it was "for show"—not that I knew what shows needed dead flowers. While she did that, I slid out from under the table and put my ear to the basement door. Daddy's workshop was down there. No one was down there right now because he was away on a business trip. That's what Mom said.

But last night, when I was in the kitchen getting a drink of water, I heard sounds coming from the basement. Dragging, slow ones. And a noise like... like bubble wrap popping inside a deep, echoey cave.

Why were things so *weird* around here lately? Maybe it was part of what Mom had planned?

I wanted to check out what was going on down there, but I had to wait for my moment. As she always did nowadays when she finished in the garden, Mom marched upstairs to shower—which is funny because she doesn't get dirty working on anything out there anymore—and I knew this was my chance. Her showers take a long time. Long enough to watch three episodes of my favorite cartoons in a row. I counted them myself.

I dragged a chair to the fridge so I could grab the silver key on top. I was good at finding hiding spots. I used it to unlock the basement door, jumping at the loud creaking sounds it seemed to be making just to tattle on me. I checked on Mom—yes, the water was still running—before going down into Dad's workshop.

The stairs were dark. The air smelled *wrong*, like yucky old yogurt. I went slowly, a tight grip on the railing with both hands. I was focused on my feet. I was scared someone might grab my ankles through the gap between each step. I saw a YouTube clip from a scary movie about that once. That's why I didn't see him until I got to the bottom.

"Daddy?"

Tied to a chair, head and shoulders slumped forward, he looked like a sad, half-deflated balloon the day after a party. He wasn't covered in blood or anything, but he sure didn't look normal. At the sound of my voice, he opened his eyes. They didn't look right either. They weren't my daddy's blue eyes. Now they were a cloudy, muddy brown—the same, strange color Mom's normally green eyes had turned three days ago.

"Buddy," he croaked. He lifted his head and tilted it to the side. I heard the popping bubble wrap sound again. The noise sounded wet down here. He had a huge, creepy, *all wrong* smile on his face. "Come down to join me?" he said, "I'm almost ready... But not...safe...you're not old enough."

Something shifted behind me. I heard more wet popping. And then—

"Sweetheart."

Mom's voice from the top of the stairs. She didn't sound mad or scared. She sounded...*wrong*.

I turned, and though I never heard her come down the stairs, she was right there in front of me. She was taller than usual. Her smile was messed up too, wide enough to show all her teeth—*too many of them*—all the way to the back. Her hands hung at her sides, fingers twitching like they were practicing how to grab me.

"You weren't supposed to see this," she said. I saw a flash of something scuttling behind her. It was small, fast, and silver, with long, shiny limbs bending at funny angles. I didn't see any hands or feet.

Mom reached out to touch me, and I ran. I bolted past her, hearing a chirping siren sound—not from her mouth, but from somewhere deeper, like a fire alarm inside her chest. I didn't stop until I was outside and five blocks away, where I couldn't hear it anymore.

The world looked normal as my feet beat the pavement. And yet *not*. Many of the neighbors were outside, all smiling. When I was sprinting for my life, I noticed Mr. Jenson was pretending to wash his car with an empty bucket. Catching my breath, I sat on the curb and watched a woman rake the same empty patch of lawn over and over. I didn't like how widely every grown-up I saw smiled, nor how often. They stood too straight and blinked too slowly.

I wished I had my backpack; it had snacks in it. But it was at my house, and I didn't dare go back. I walked to my best friend Georgie Abershene's house instead. Their yard backed up to the woods, where we had a secret fort. I planned to spend the night in it, and maybe Georgie would go with me.

His house was a single-story, so I snuck up to his bedroom window. I saw my bestie reading comics on his bedspread. My knuckles were about to rap on the glass to get his attention when Mr. Abershene knocked on his door and stood in the hallway asking, "Hey, little big man. You haven't seen Buddy today, have you? His mother called, looking for him."

Georgie looked up from his reading. "No, sir. Maybe he's at Jamal's house."

"Come to the table. It's time for dinner."

I froze. Georgie didn't seem to suspect anything yet, but I could see that his dad didn't look right. How could my friend not notice that his father's shirt was inside out and backwards? His parents were like the rest of them. I backed away from the window and fled to the woods, to our tented safehouse. Maybe Georgie would find me there later, and I can tell him everything.

I stole food from my friends' houses when no one was home. Stuff that didn't go in the fridge, of course. For three days, I tried not to be seen while I watched grown-ups go house to house, ringing doorbells and getting welcomed inside some of them. Each day, more neighbors joined them. More doors opened.

It would soon be harder to hide. Maybe I was just four years old, but I wasn't stupid. I couldn't sit in the dark, sheltered from the rain in this fort, forever. Winter and its cold weather were coming, and then what? I pressed my face into my arms to stifle the sound of my crying. That's when I heard snapping twigs. Many twigs, many feet—I knew what I was hearing.

I thought if I stayed small and quiet, they wouldn't notice me. But I inched back the flap of the entrance and peeked.

Mom stood in the clearing. Waiting. Smiling. Tilting her head at me, the way our chickens did when they found something they wanted to eat. In the twilight through the trees, I saw other grown-ups standing behind her.

I thought, *Did they know where I was the whole time?*

Wider and wider, their smiles stretched. Their footsteps hastened across the wet grass as they came for me.

Foiling Feline

DR. DEAD ZONE LOOMS over his workstation, fingers poised for pursuing world domination, one evil act at a time.

Just a few more keystrokes, he thinks, eyes alight with glee behind his absurdly reflective goggles. *With this, every city's traffic light will turn green simultaneously. Chaos. Glorious gridlock chaos!*

The Doomsday Determiner dashboard pings behind him. "Execute Global Protocol: MeowMix.v87?" it asks.

The mad doctor turns. "What the—?"

A furry orange minion sits on the DD's console. Whiskers twitching. Tail bushy.

"Derkis! No!"

But the cat (full name: Derkis von Paws III, informal title: Lord of Naps) has plans of his own. With a majestic stretch and complete disregard for supervillainy, he sashays across the keyboard as if it were a catwalk in Milan.

Dr. Dead Zone lunges for him.

Too late!

Derkis strikes the [ENTER] key to confirm the command.

No streetlight patterns change. Instead, every screen across the globe—whether a personal device in a home or a brightly lit digital billboard—changes over to a slideshow of Doctor Dead Zone's baby photos. Synced to Celine Dion and signed by @DerkisTheCatLord.

"Oh no!" The doctor grabs fistfuls of his own hair and yanks, feeling a wave of humiliation crash over him. "*Not the tutu ones.*"

Across continents, people stop what they are doing and go *OooOoo* and *Awwww*. Teenagers upload tribute TikTok videos. Kelly Clarkson's show is interrupted when the Baby Dead Zone hack plays on the screen behind her and Jason Momoa, right in the middle of his answering her poignant question about acting with children.

#FluffyOverlord #WhiskerWins #CoupDeMeow

The mad-now-humiliated doctor collapses into his swivel chair, defeated not by heroes—nor by lasers or meddling kids—but by pink, little toe beans. He glares at Derkis, now displaying his skills at licking his own butthole.

"You do realize," he mutters, "you've ruined my big reveal with a meme."

With slow and deliberate eyelids, the ring-tailed tabby blinks in response, then sends his human's energy drink crashing to the floor with one sweeping paw.

"I'll get you for this, fur-brains!"

Derkis von Paws III's deftness is unmatched. Avoiding Dr. Dead Zone's angry hands, he leaps up onto the ventilation rafters, out of reach, and yawns. Pleased with today's results, he wonders what tomorrow's plan will do to the doctor's sanity.

Nanobot Noodle Soup for the Soulless

Felicia and Michelle settled onto the loveseat, a tub of ice cream and two spoons between them. They were about to stream their favorite show when Felicia switched over to the nightly news brief first.

On the television screen, two news anchors were smiling. The woman's version came off a bit stiff, and the man grinned like he had rehearsed it all morning in the mirror.

"Good evening, I'm Christina Chastain."

"And I'm Joe Carver. Tonight's top story: biotech startup HumanCore says their latest empathy nanobots are, and I quote, 'unlocking emotional intelligence for the emotionally bankrupt.'"

Christina nodded. "Dubbed *Project SoulSoup*, the nanobots are delivered via a designer consommé priced at $57,000 per spoonful. We asked CEO Brexlyn Donavan if this was satire. In her response, she said, 'Only poor people think irony is free.' What are the people saying about this, Joe?"

Joe chuckled. "Reviews are pouring in. Per billionaire hedge fund manager Kaylie Dunbard's tweet: 'Cried during a Folgers commercial. Hugged my barista. Tipped 32%!' What do you think about that, Christina?"

"That's progress, I guess."

Reading from a teleprompter off-screen, Joe continued. "But some users report complications. Take a look at this post from Mandy Mitz @LadyLamboLegs, heiress to the synthetic champagne empire."

The newscasters were replaced by a TikTok video featuring footage of a cute squirrel stockpiling food on a leaf pile inside its shelter, unaware of hidden cameras filming it. After a few seconds of this, it cut to a sobbing, redheaded woman in a purple ball gown. Heavy rivers of mascara flowed from her eyes. A party of some sort was continuing around her unnoticed. It was the heiress herself who, between gasps and sobs, managed to say, "He buries all his nuts! Just like... just like Daddy buries his feelings!"

The screen swapped back to the broadcast studio. Her voice serious, Christina read from her own set of scrolling text. "HumanCore admits side effects may include hallucinations of past moral infractions, such as hearing the cries of underpaid laborers in their wallpaper or seeing the ghosts of endangered animals in the luxury sauna steam."

Joe chimed in. "We spoke with Dr. Vinya Patel, neuroethics expert at Oxford. Take a look."

Once more, the screen transitioned to a pre-taped reel, this time of Dr. Patel, who seemed unimpressed by the whole thing. "They've essentially outsourced a conscience," he was saying.

"It's less 'awakening the soul' and more 'installing guilt with firmware updates,' if you ask me. But here we are."

Back in the studio, Christina pressed on with the story. "Despite criticism, pre-orders for the Gold Reserve batch—engineered to simulate remorse for infidelity and crimes against humanity—sold out in less than five minutes."

"No word yet on the rumored Budget Empathy Lite option for the middle class, which insiders say is in the works," Joe added.

The woman anchor smiled into the camera. "Up next: Is your Roomba judging your lifestyle? Could they be sharing your personal lives with others? A Stream-Channel 9 investigation."

Joe stacked and straightened his papers without any real meaning, an action he does every night. "But first, a message from our sponsors... HumanCore: Because even the soulless deserve a good cry."

A small laugh from Christina. "Don't they, though?"

The broadcast went to a commercial break. Michelle took the controller from Felicia and changed to the streaming channel playing their favorite show, *Apocalypse Vs. Babysitters Brigade.* They settled in for the night.

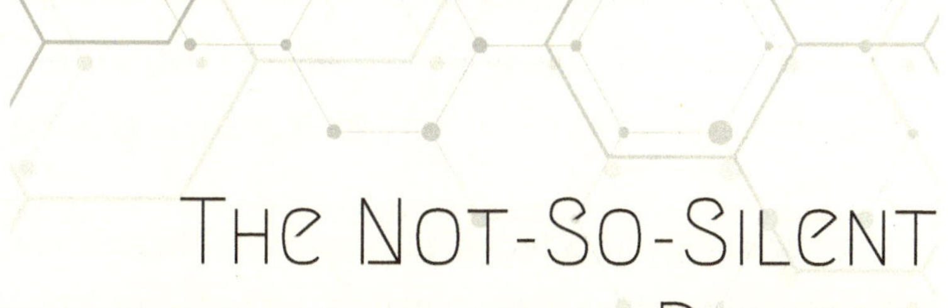

The Not-So-Silent Panels

So maybe Melanie is nonverbal, but she *draws.*

She doodles in the mornings, before school hours. She draws in the afternoons, when the house is quiet except for the rustle of pages and sounds from her parents cooking dinner or watching TV. She creates panels—sometimes neat, sometimes experimental—with an eerie, skillful precision that makes the hair on her mother's arms stick up.

Today's comic is four pages. No words. Just inked actions.

Panel one: A boy in a green hoodie stands on the train tracks that run alongside Elmhurst Street. His mother is shown down the block. She's rushing to reach her adventurous son, who had gotten away from her. But it looks like she's too far away...

Panel two: A blur of a sneaker on gravel, a backpack rolling down the slope.

Panel three: Melanie's dad, sprinting at full speed.

Panel four: The boy, safe and sitting on the curb, crying but alive. He's in the arms of his hysterical, grateful mother.

Melanie's mother looks over them. "Another one," she calls to her husband. She hands the pages to him; he grabs his keys and his shoes, reviewing the artwork while he hustles his way to the car.

They have long since stopped questioning it. The first time she made a prediction, they thought it was a coincidence. They felt no blame when it came to be—how were they to know?—but they will always regret not acting sooner after the second time. When the third opportunity came around, Melanie's drawing of a living room fire led them to their neighbor's house minutes after a faulty Christmas tree light sparked, and they understood. Melanie isn't limited to sketching what she thinks or worries about; she can see what *will be.*

The morning after the neighbor's holiday incident made the local news, she drew again. No tragedy this time.

Panel one: Melanie's mother is in the kitchen, stirring up cups of cocoa for everyone—extra marshmallows all around.

Panel two: Her father is humming, getting the TV ready for Melanie's favorite movie, *Puss in Boots.*

Panel three: The three of them on the couch, Melanie tucked between, wrapped in a weighted blanket down to her knees.

Panel four: Her parents, both looking down at her as they tuck her into bed.

That night played out exactly as shown.

Melanie's parents don't need prompting. They act on the foresight depictions without question. But some do not depict an immediate future. Once, her mom found a single panel taped to the fridge: an adult Melanie standing in a fancy art gallery;

her drawings are framed in glass, attached to price tags with large numbers.

Melanie often draws herself as she is now—small and seated—in one panel, and besides that, another box featuring an older warrior-girl wielding a pen like a sword with her parents behind her.

Words are rarely used in her comics.
But in her stories, she says a lot.

Memory Meets Man Again

Hey, nice to see you again.
Are you doing as well as you were back then?
Even though it's been quite a while,
Cute musty old memories of us still meander
Through the part of my mind
Where I used to have that happy place.
And when I do think of you,
A shadow of a smile finds my face
Because I can only remember
The best left behind:
The kisses filled with silky love,
The closeness of our hips,
And the laughter, light as lace.
Not a bit of bad can chase
That faint expression that found my lips.

It's so nice to hear your voice.
I still wear the ring you gave me.

And, yes, I know you're far—God, so far—gone from me.
But around my neck on its chain remains an icon
That reminds me of what's been lost after my poor choice.
Truthfully, I'm still quite lonely
Even in a crowded square,
With all the attention on me.
On stage, I still catch myself glancing over beside me,
Only to remember you're not there
And no longer shall you be.

But really, what I have to say
Before you walk away
Is that I hope you smile, too.
Do you, when you think of me and you?
At a thought of what we had,
I hope the feeling is more sweet than sad.
Yes, I can see you have somewhere else to be,
But do me a little favor for me as you depart:
Smile for me and my aching heart.

The Margins Are Closing In

It started with a Post-it note on the fridge.

DON'T TRUST THE MIRROR. IT'S RECORDING!

Dorothy blinked at her own looping handwriting. Her signature swirl on the *s*—there was no doubt. But she hadn't written it. She *hadn't.* She would have remembered a crazy thing like that. Her doctor said her memory was "reasonably intact for someone in her condition," and encouraged her to do daily crossword puzzles to help her keep it that way for as long as possible. She resided independently in a small apartment in an assisted living center, with no plans to move upstairs to the memory care unit anytime soon.

Later that day, in the snack alcove, she found another.

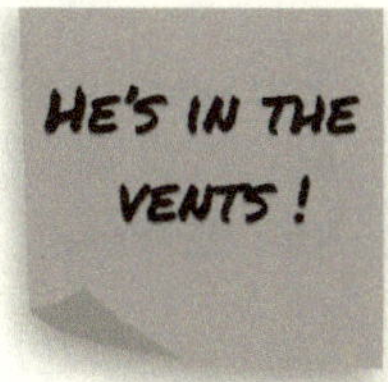

There was no *he* in her life. Not anymore. All of her sons were grown, moved far away, with adult children of their own, as a matter of fact. Her second late husband, Hal, would have laughed at the absurdity of this note—then check the vents to make her feel better.

But she could check for herself, couldn't she? And she *did* check. There was evidence of mouse activity and little else.

The notes kept coming. She started collecting them in a shoebox, organizing them like crime scene evidence. Each in her handwriting, though unsigned.

Returning after Monday's Bingo night, she spotted one in the kitchen.

ASK WHAT HE
DID WITH ALL
THE JEWELRY.

On Wednesday, she discovered one in the shower.

YOU'RE NOT
IMAGINING
THE SMELL.

She found another tucked into the pocket of her housecoat.

YOU'RE NOT
IMAGINING
THE SMELL.

That night, Dorothy tried lying perfectly still, eyes half-lidded. She wondered if she was going crazy and fell asleep contemplating the answer to that.

She lost track of time for a few days. She sometimes thought it was 1990, mistaking her two-room unit for the hotel she shared with her best friends, Susie and Tiffany, during their high school theater trip to Los Angeles. She occasionally worried that she was falling behind on grading her children's assignments. These hazy moments came and went. Usually, no one had to remind her that she cashed in on her pension ages ago; she came around to it on her own after a while.

It was Sunday when the phone call came, 2:58 p.m. Dorothy answered. Silence on the other end, and then her own small, far-away voice.

"Stop collecting them. They'll catch on."

After the line went dead, Dorothy sat motionless on the couch for what felt like hours. She checked her incoming call history. There had been no call.

She chose not to message the doctor's office. Not yet. She didn't tell the resident nurses, her neighbors, or her family. She opened her desk drawer instead and retrieved a stack of blank stationery. She sat down and wrote:

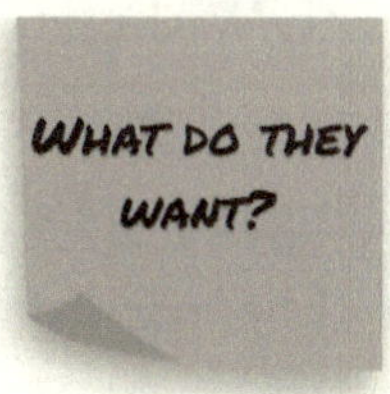

She tucked the slip of paper beneath the sugar bowl. It was gone in the morning, a new one in its place.

The day she found one of the notes taped to her forehead was the day she finally understood everything.

They weren't warnings. They were *reminders*. Not for things she forgot. Of things she wasn't *supposed* to remember. Yes, she was dealing with the early stages of dementia, but this wasn't about the illness, not completely. Something *else* had been trying to get through. Parts of her brain lived in healthier gray matter regions, and *those* parts had been leaving breadcrumbs.

She remembered that she did more than retire as a science teacher in Wilkes County, Washington; she had also served twelve years as an operative ecologist for the CIA after her time in the classroom. Her colleagues were accustomed to her writing messages in the margins of her printed reports. The note taped to her head was the last trigger to a lost memory.

It had been a foggy Tuesday morning. She was conducting fieldwork in Tuckaw County that week, gathering samples from water sources miles from civilization. Her bosses suspected the local plant might be contaminating the ecosystem. The terrain was strenuous, steep slopes rising and falling away. And it was *wet*. A rainstorm had swept through the area the weekend before. The ground washed out from under her when she crested a hill overlooking a nasty, rocky decline. That's why she slipped and tumbled all the way down the embankment—well, that and she had been running in a blind panic.

She checked herself for broken bones and head injuries and found she was bleeding from the temple. She felt dazed. Truth be told, she had felt confused earlier that day, while in line for the hotel lobby's continental breakfast bar. And if she stayed on this honesty train, she'd have to admit that those hazy, forgetful moments had been springing up on her all summer. Coupled with the head trauma from the fall, that disorienting cloud crept up ten times stronger as she stumbled through rows of trees.

"And what you were running from in the first place?" Dorothy asked herself, sitting on the edge of her couch, gazing down at the latest Post-it note.

A thought formed: *I stumbled on a gruesome scene, a* deadly *secret.*

Before her fall, Dorothy had wandered off course in her sample-gathering. Not a lot and not on purpose, but she ended up on private property belonging to a man named Herbert Schewel, according to the Parcel GPS app on her government-issued phone. She took a different, windier path on her trek off his land, wanting to avoid walking up the particularly difficult hill she had come down here on. That's the only reason she happened upon the massive dumpsite of bodies in his woods.

Massive somehow felt like an undeserving word for the horrific sight that Dorothy's shocked face beheld. It was clear that the storm caused a washout in these parts, thereby unearthing countless victims in various stages of decomposition. And oh, the *smell*. It seemed to her that this sickening odor would haunt her senses until her own death. She felt dizzy.

I can't be found here, she recalled thinking as she stood there surveying the horror. Blind panic overrode her mind then, and it was her legs that took over from there. She never even saw that embankment with its rocky drop coming until she was below it.

Fourteen hours later, she had wandered out of the woods and into a Harvey's Truck Stop, where she made it as far as the stunned man at the register before passing out. She couldn't tell paramedics what her name was, where she lived, or where she'd been. And while knowledge of her life (like her identity and her job) did return, she never recovered any memories from the last three weeks before the hospital. It was there that doctors and social workers had given her the full report on a diagnosis she had been so successfully avoiding until then.

The authorities would have considered Dorothy's terrific discovery crucial information two years ago if she had been able to remember it. If only the first heavy signs of mental decline hadn't reared their ugly heads on her last mission. But the timing was more critical now, she was sure of it. The reason for what kick-started the return of these memories was crystal clear to her. It was the campaign ad repeatedly playing on TV that did it, the one endorsing a certain Mr. Schewel who was running for Governor in this year's election.

Dorothy left her apartment in Holly Hills, the assisted living community she'd been living in since her medically dictated retirement. She did not leave a note. Cameras captured her exiting the facility, talking on her cellphone. She appeared to be in a hurry.

And, of course, she was! After all, she wasn't sure how much time she had left before she forgot again.

Dear Mom, From the Clone Who Didn't Turn Out Evil

Hi, Mom.

It's me, Batch 27. You said you'd call me "Leo" if I turned out stable, so... Hi, it's me, your son Leo.

I heard about the latest incident. First of all, *yikes!* Second, I had nothing to do with the teleportation accident at the Capitol last month. Honestly, I haven't figured out teleportation technology. I can get the printer to connect to my tablet, and that's the extent of it.

Look, Mom, I get it; the track record's... not great. Out of thirty-five cloned children, the results aren't in my favor. You tried your best, you really did, but let's face it: for most of us, nature *and* nurture both packed their bags and moved to Vegas.

But me? I'm *good*.

My eyes don't glow. I don't breathe fire. I don't hear people's thoughts unless they're *really* loud (and it's usually about sex or sandwiches). I have no desire to "enslave humanity" or "found a

New Dynasty under a blood-red sky" or whatever it is Max #3 is posting on HoloFlitter these days.

I want to paint BattleCast figurines and hang out with my friends on Wednesday nights. You told us you dreamed that one of us would enjoy a quiet life. Remember? You said, "If you turn out boring, I will be the proudest mother in the galaxy."

Well, Mom, have I got news for you! I am *extremely boring.* I'm an accountant—that's how boring! It's an art form, really. Today, for example, I made a sandwich (roast beef, one slice of pickle, minimal condiments for optimal bread integrity), then spent four hours painting the tiny plasma canisters on my miniature ship models. I have a thrilling weekend planned: I'm reorganizing my spice rack alphabetically *and* by heat index. (Spicy → Mild, in case you were wondering.)

I'm writing because... well, I guess I'm worried. After what happened with Solomon #5 last week (it crushed me to learn the extent of the tsunami's damage), I know the government is suggesting a Total Recall Order.

That would include me, Mom. And I'm not a threat to anybody.

I know I'm a clone, and I know that freaks people out. Even nice people. And you, sometimes. You get that look. The one that says: *Which version are you? Can I trust you?*

And I get it. I do. Trust is hard when your other "sons" have razed half of New Prague or tried to crash the Colony Nine station into the moon. But I'm still me. I like chamomile tea. I find violent movies to be too stressful. I'm the sweet iteration in my group who, when you gave us our first robotics kits for Christmas, made a mechanical bird feeder instead of a weapon.

I'm the one who never tried to mind-control the neighbors, even when Mr. Stevenson wouldn't stop programming his lawn mower to start at 4 a.m. (I hear his wife passed on, by the way. Please send my best condolences to him and his daughter.) I'm Leo, the son who made you a hand-painted Mother's Day mug that says "#1 Mom (Genetic Source)" and meant it with all my weird little copy-heart.

I don't need a throne. I don't want a spaceship or an armada—or a spaceship armada. What *is* on my wishlist is my own holographic trading card series, and to keep living my unremarkable and *peaceful*, paint-splattered life. Maybe meet someone nice. I was thinking about adopting a dog and naming him something old-fashioned like Harold. Dogs deserve solid names, not all that baby babble nonsense.

So if it comes to a vote, Mom—when you're sitting there with the other members of the Council, fingers hovering over that decision button—remember me. Not my duplicated doppelgängers. Please think of the son who didn't blow anything up, who didn't demand the world bow to him—the only clone who didn't turn out evil.

Please don't lump me in with them. Please believe in me the way you believed in the original mission behind your project, back when you had hope in your eyes and burnt toast on your plate because you were too busy studying gene sequences to eat properly. You wanted to build a better future. My siblings lost sight of that, ran wild and scary because they thought being "better" meant being "bigger" or "louder" or "shinier." I don't know why they never grew past that. To me, being "the best" looks like being kind and boring on purpose.

I love you, Mom. I want to be here. Come over and join my friends and me. We make enough tea and cookies for everyone.

Your son [the GOOD one],
Leo

P.S.—Tell Mr. Svenson I'm sorry about the note I left on his mower when I was five. I called it a "harbinger of dawn-based despair," and I shouldn't have done that. I was having a poetic day, but it's no excuse.

No Vacancy (For Terror)

Reputed to be the most feared address east of the Mississippi, the Henry Basselman House had a reputation for driving men to flee, landing women in the institution, and corrupting the youth. Ah, but nothing lasts forever. In 2015, the worst thing imaginable happened. It became an Airbnb listing. This brought the dreaded Influencers.

The nights fell into sameness. The house endured the same ritual: guests live-stream their stay while drinking White Claws and wearing matching monogrammed robes. Ghost-hunting TikTokers arranged EMF meters like centerpieces. The real poltergeist who lived there was on a rotating schedule for autographs.

The house was *livid*.

It threw lamps; they said it had "cottagegore vibes." Its floorboards groaned without the provocation of a footstep. Faucets dripped blood. Mirrors fogged with profanity. Yet the visitors beamed at the special effects.

Enough was enough. Disrespected, underappreciated, and desperate, the supernatural property tried something new. The poltergeist helped it book a meeting with a medium—one boasting a five-star Yelp rating. Times have changed.

"This isn't a possession problem," Madame Sona said, tapping her bejeweled acrylics against a teacup. "*This* is an identity crisis."

"I used to *scare* people, damn it," the house wailed. The walls rattled from its high volume. "Behold the grand haunt, reduced to a backdrop for engagement photos!"

"Then it's time," she intoned, "to *rebrand*."

The new marketing strategy reshaped the website's homepage.

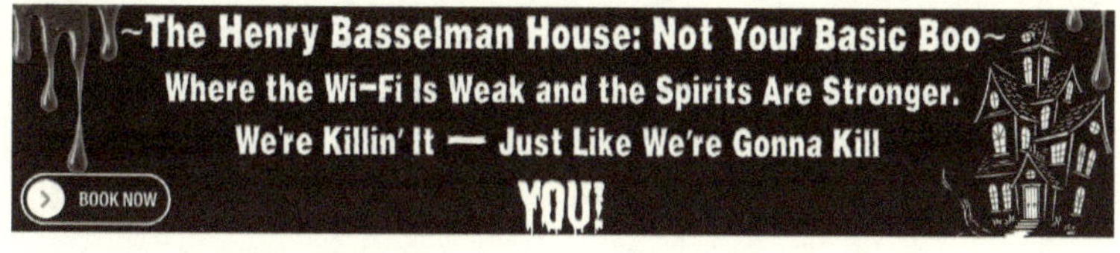

No more pillow mints. No more ghost tours with themed cocktails. The house went feral. Beds levitated. Walls bled Latin phrases. Victorian children sobbed, a chorus of 3D surround sound experiences. The reviews and comments were spectacular.

> "This place is unhinged—five stars!"
>
> [The Bindhi Family]

> "Finally, a haunting with guts (literally)."
>
> [Spook Team 6]

"My boyfriend's still possessed. Booking again next year!"

[Petra Inglewood]

The Henry Basselman House sighed, defeated. It gave up and gave in, and the attic's proudest poltergeist updated his résumé to reflect his new accomplishments.

Fangs and Hickory Heart

IT IS MY BELIEF that a person can't help but reveal who they are between the hours of 3 and 5 in the morning. I've observed plenty of evidence of this.

Some folks are tucked in bed, clinging to the dreams they are havin'. Others—the youthful ones, usually—are stumblin' home (entwined with another, if they got lucky) after last call at one of the many bars in town. But me? I'm elbow-deep in brisket rub and low on patience for romantic nonsense, which is why initially I didn't think much of the tall, pale stranger who wandered up to my row of smokers. He appeared from the narrow, shadowy alley that slices between Hickory Heart (my to-go restaurant) and my neighbor's cute little saloon that favors southern rock performances. I figured he was drunk, lost, or both. Possibly looking for trouble.

This is Texas, after all.

"What *is* that irresistible scent?" he asked, voice smooth and thick like gravy, attractive and foreign.

"Smoke. Meat. Hard work. Take your pick," I replied without looking up at him a second time.

Not born yesterday, I tracked his movements in my peripheral vision. I appeared to be in the zone, tending to my sacred trinity: brisket, ribs, and sausage. My gloved hands were covered in seasoning, determination set into my face as I rubbed it into a rack of ribs. A meat thermometer was strapped to my apron like a pistol, but my real gun was ready (should I need it) in its holster on the other side. If it turned out to be food he was after, I had a tray of jalapeño cheddar cornbread cooling on the little square picnic table behind me that should satisfy him.

He didn't laugh at my joke, choosing to hover in front of the first smoker like it was prey. Odd for a city boy, based on the fashion he wore, to know the shape of hunger so well as to ask strangers behind an alley for food.

"Beef or pork?" he asked.

"Brisket. Black Angus. Dry rub with espresso, brown sugar, ancho chili. Y'want a bite or a sermon?"

He smiled. Lord, that smile was too clean for someone nosing around a backdoor BBQ pit before dawn. "You cook with life and vigor," he said. "I can taste it in the air."

I liked that. And I could listen to that accent all day. European? Ah, but Europe is a big place, ain't it? It sounded *old*, though.

On an unfamiliar impulse, I offered him a stool. "You a food critic or a poetic weirdo in a nice vest?"

"Just a man with cravings."

That made me pause. I've had my share of oddballs drop by over the years. Drifters with nowhere to be. Influencers looking for gritty aesthetic content. But this one? He was quiet. There was a stillness about him. Like the air in the eye of a summer storm before it rolls past.

"You always this much of an early bird, sir?" I asked. "Because I'm closed until six, for the breakfast crowd."

"I prefer the night."

"Then why ya sniffin' my ribs instead of howlin' at the moon?"

He looked amused. "Because I smelled something divine."

"Ah. That'll be my Peach-Bottom Bourbon BBQ glaze comin' out of that there cooker. Pairs well with dead animals and other poor dietary decisions."

That one *did* get a laugh. Happy, dark, and natural like he'd been doing it for a few centuries. We sat in silence as the sensual deliciousness in the air from the meat intensified. He watched me with stunning old-cellar-colored eyes, cool and gray. I offered him a burnt end, a Midwest custom, warm from my own breakfast not twenty minutes ago. Business owners: the real early birds who catch the worm, ya better believe it.

He chewed with his eyes closed. Cute crinkles, barely wrinkles, formed in the corners of those eyes. *Damn your genetics*, I remember thinking to myself, because he looked like he could be as young as thirty-five or as old as fifty-five, closer to my age. I watched him the way a curious hawk regards a rattler.

"Well?" I asked. Despite the quirkiness of the situation, I wanted his opinion. Burnt ends were my favorite.

He opened his eyes. "Savory. Sweet. That whisper-lick of flame. You cook like someone who understands hunger."

"Yeah. I reckon I do."

That's when he leaned forward, and I noticed the way his eyes caught the light in a different way than normal folks. And the way his skin didn't bead up with sweat like mine did. "And what do you know about hunger?" he asked.

I shrugged. "Enough to fear it and feed it in others."

He nodded, impressed with my answer. "Most people don't understand. Hunger is a language. A mean one. It speaks in cravings. Some chase sugar, others salt. Some want flesh. Everybody hungers for something, but rarely has one truly experienced *real hunger.*"

He looked at me like someone who knew my name already. Maybe he knew my mother's name, too—God rest her soul, whichever end it turned up in—and everything else about my life. And still I wasn't scared, though I should have been.

"Flesh, huh?" I asked, confident he was making macabre jokes about barbecuing animals and feeding them to people for a living, and finding that I wished to volley one back. "So you eat people or just creep them out?"

That earned another chuckle. "Not unless invited."

I studied him. He was either being very clever in our banter or incredibly forward. "Well, I'd say you're two metaphors away from making me suspicious."

"Are you afraid of me?"

"I handle dead things for a living. Butcher them up. You think I'm scared of a man with attractive cheekbones and dramatic entrances?"

"Do you want to know what I am?"

"No," I said, with as much sass as the Carolina Gold Ghost Pepper sauce I had smothered onto another piece of meat. "I want to know if you can handle the heat."

My special recipe makes grown men weep. I've witnessed it many times. I offered it to him speared to the end of my fork. He bit in, not breaking eye contact with me. And then, as if caught off guard, he closed his eyes again—this time in absolute reverence.

I felt... proud? Something. I felt *something*, and it was akin to ego and temptation. I offered him a bottle of water from the cooler under the table. While he drank from it, I whipped out my vape pen containing a concentrated concoction of Pineapple Kush. We continue to regard each other over the objects in our hands.

"You spice like someone who's suffered."

"Everyone suffers. Some of us smoke through it," I joked, waving my weed stick back and forth in a teensy wave with one hand and using a fork with the other to spear another chunk of smoked meat. Show me a man who doesn't like puns, and I'll say to you that man's a problem in your life.

That was when he looked me square in the eye and held me there. "You ever wish you could make it last forever? The flavor. Life. Everything?"

And that... that was when I should've known. You don't have to murmur it to yourself. I'm aware of how dumb I look in that segment of time. But you see, we don't always recognize when it's happenin'—that pivotal turn, that moment when our reality is about to change. I thought this was a *regular,* strange encounter at my pit. I didn't know I was bartering with my fate.

The sky was beginning to pinken at the edges. The stranger stood.

"I must go," he said. "But I will return. If I may?"

I nodded. "If you bring the fine wine."

A few minutes after he left, it was like a fog had lifted. I realized, feeling slow, that he never said his name. And I never asked for it. I *should* have flinched at that. I know that—don't rub it in.

But I'll have you know, I remembered to ask his name during our second encounter. Gheorghe—that's his name, pronounced like *George* but spelled weird in the old school Romanian way—returned for several nights, taste-testing my food as if it were sacrosanct. It didn't get any less mysterious each time, but I began to feel as though he was courting me.

When I served him a plate of lamb chops that had spent all of thirty seconds on the grill, he moaned. *A deep moan.* It caused me to lean across the table—in a shocking series of involuntary actions, mind you—to grasp his hands and declare, "I wish I could watch you flirt with my spice rubs for an eternity."

For a microsecond, he looked startled by my words. Then his features were delighted. "Do you understand what you're asking?"

I did. And I didn't. But I said yes either way, and that's all that matters.

Now, listen. People—they're fascinated by what it's like to be turned into a vampire. They imagine it's romantic. Tragic. *Sexy.*

It's not. It's hunger. Pure and molten and eternal. You feel every blood cell in your body flare with fire. Every nerve ending screams out. Your last breath tastes like smoke and surrender.

And when it's over—truly over—you wake up with a craving deeper than a gravesite at the bottom of a volcano.

The first thing I did in my new everlasting life was bite into a peach from the bowl on the counter. It tasted like sunlight. Then I tasted Gheorghe (only the once), and he too tasted sweet, but like a storm. We spent a little over five decades together—traveling, cooking, feeding—before I tried parting ways for fresher experiences in our undead routines.

If I'm bein' honest, I knew even before he refused to let me leave him that the wish I made all those years ago would be so literal.

So I still smoke at 3 a.m.

The Importance of Taking Turns

At seven, Mia didn't know what it meant to give something up. Not really. Her world was still packed-lunch-predictable—literally. PB&J (crust off), salt and vinegar chips, a chocolate chip cookie, and a folded note from Mom.

The swing was hers. She'd waited through most of recess for her turn with it. And now, sneaker toes digging into the mulch and hands on the chains, she was ready to fly.

That's when the new kid shuffled into Mia's field of vision. Tall. Only a little older than she was, but she didn't know his name. He wore a hand-me-down green polo shirt and faded jeans, and because his older brothers were larger than he was, they were baggy on him. He kept his hands in his pockets and his eyes on the ground.

Kids parted around him as if he were made of noobie-cooties. The boy eyed the swing with excitement, too shy to ask for a turn for the past three visits to the playground. He turned to go back the way he came, shoulders already folding in on themselves.

Mia held on to both chains, hesitated, then let go. "New Kid! Wait. You can have a turn if you want to."

There wasn't a thank you as far as words go—just a happy, excited nod, which was plenty good enough. Mia watched the new kid swing higher than the other kids dared and wondered if he would flip over the top. She couldn't pinpoint why she gave up her spot, only that something about the boy touched her heart in the same way that seeing other children hug their moms made her sad.

The boy's name was Kal, and they spent all their time together at the playground because it wasn't until high school that they shared any classes. Then they began habitually swapping playlists—songs they passed back and forth like secret notes. Those exchanges led to more intimate slice-of-life moments that stitched their life together.

A week before their graduation, Mia stood beside Kal at the foot of the front steps leading out of the school.

"Do you remember that day we met?" Kal asked.

Mia smiled. "The swing? Yeah. I thought you were going to loop over the top."

"I was scared of what would happen if I did."

Mia glanced at him. A far cry from the scrawny boy she first met, he now filled out his own broad shadow and wore his paint-stained backpack with pride. When Mia's ground shook, his gaze always steadied her.

"You came back to Earth, though," Mia said. "And stayed there."

Kal bumped her shoulder. "Because you made room."

If a God-like observer were to flip past the calendar pages a few years, they could stop at the backyard barbecue beneath a giant "Happy 5th Birthday, Mikala!" banner to find a smiling Mia watching Kal as he pushes their daughter on a swing, her little legs kicking at the sky.

All Mia did was give up her turn. And somehow, it turned into everything.

The Burglar and the Sleepwalker

It was supposed to be an uncomplicated robbery. One lock. One sleeping, medicated old man. One more haul before the streetlights gave up their last golden rays of protection.

The burglar (whose name, for the sake of this story, is Aaron) prided himself on professionalism. His mother had once told him, "If you're going to sin, at least do it with good posture." He'd taken that to heart.

Aaron's entrance was silent, as they always were, but he made it five steps into the home when he heard the faint scuff of slippers whispering against wood. He froze.

A figure emerged from the darkness that shadowed the end of the hall—an elderly individual in blue pajamas patterned with tiny sailboats. His eyes were closed to slits, yet his face was turned toward Aaron with unsettling precision. Aaron jumped in surprise, swallowing a lump in his throat that he suspected was his own heart. He started to run for it, had even lurched his body halfway back the way he came, when he realized this homeowner was still asleep, just as he was supposed to be.

"You came back home," the sleepwalking old man (let's call him Wally) murmured.

Aaron had, regrettably, left his script for this situation at home. "Errr... yes?"

"Come on then," Wally said, brushing past Aaron, who followed more out of curiosity and less because he wanted to. And anyway, the old geezer might sleep-lead him to something valuable.

Framed photographs colonized the living room walls: sepia portraits in ornate frames, Polaroids curling at the edges, and crisper digital prints. The vibe of the gallery was "honoring the family tree." Wally gestured to a young man in one of the oldest Polaroids. He had a soft-focus smile, and he wore a wide-brimmed fedora that complemented his salmon-colored "Sunday Best" suit.

"You wore this to the picnic," Wally said. "My sister said the hat was ridiculous, but I said it made you the hero of a novel no one's written yet."

Aaron, who had been told many things in his life but never that he resembled a romantic protagonist, said nothing.

"You never did like your picture taken," the man went on. "But I took it anyway. I knew one day I'd need proof."

Proof of what, Aaron didn't ask. There was something about the way the sleepwalker's old paper voice thinned at the edges that made questions feel cruel. The slow tour through time continued.

Wally lingered before a picture of two blurred, embracing figures in mid-spin. "We danced every night, one song before bed," he said. "You always hummed the tune before I put the record on."

Aaron felt the strange dislocation of someone walking through a different life, witnessing each memory frozen in time. As the two of them reached a gap in the storytelling—a large window partially covered by a sheer white curtain—the moonlight played across Wally's sleepwalking face. It had a warm, soothing effect on him.

After a long, satisfied sigh, he commented on the lateness of the hour and shuffled to the only door left ajar, which any guest on the tour would presume to be the master bedroom. Aaron kept following. The old man climbed into his bed without hesitation and lay curled on his side, a comma waiting for the next clause. The burglar, a man who had never in his whole life tucked anyone into bed (and certainly not mid-felony), pulled a blanket over Wally's snoozing form with a care that startled him.

"Sleep well," Aaron said.

The old man, on his way to dreamland, murmured one last thing. "Always do, when you're here."

Aaron lingered in the darkened room. The loot he planned on taking was still waiting for him. He left them untouched.

Outside, the night air felt different. As he walked away to his van across the street, he thought about how easy it was to take something from someone, and how it was so much harder for him to give something back.

Aaron never broke into another house again—not because he feared being caught, but because he'd once been mistaken for someone worth missing. And that, he found, was worth more than anything he'd ever stolen.

Middle of No-Time

Please don't stop and ponder,
Just feel each and every star
That we are walking under.
It's so dark and unsure along this road right now,
With danger and romance
As both sides of this fine line.
Only us...
In the middle of no-time.

Here, tonight, hours past sunset
And closer to sunrise,
Hushed heartbeats and the evening heat
Offer such a charming quiet.
My tumbling theoretical thoughts
Come out in a voice of only human sighs.
Insecure intuitive rhetoric has taught me
To rejoice in a thousand other signs.

You're worried about what you're saying
And not on what you want me to hear.

With enlightenment on this sylvan paved path drawing near,
It's just us...
Interlacing fingers that align
In the middle of no-time.

We are ambling along these lasting yellow lines
Because we don't know how to read the language
On any of the signposts;
So my own sigh matches yours.
All this sensibility and obvious air,
Funny how everything is as it was before.

So far to join us...
Confused responsibility and a lot of care.
Are we alone then, in this design?
Is it...
Just us...
In the middle of no-time?

The Day I Blinked Wrong and Teleported

NEVER HAVE I EVER fallen asleep on the job before. To do so would risk more than my life was worth.

Yet there I was, leaning against the cold stone of the Palacio del Gobernador in Manila as the weight of the night watch dragged my eyelids shut. So heavy was my exhaustion that I felt dizzy and ill when I tried to gain control over it. You need to understand that the palace was in a state of great alarm. The night before, we received word that Chinese pirates managed to assassinate our governor, Gómez Pérez Dasmariñas, while he was away at sea and far from the safety of his home here in the Philippines. Because he was also a Spanish politician, diplomat, military officer, and a member of the Order of Santiago, tension coiled through the air like a restless, nearly invisible serpent. No one slept; everyone was on high alert until the higher authorities appointed a new governor.

I remember leaning against the wall, fighting the *mareo* I felt. I swear—I closed my eyes for only a moment. It felt like that, anyway…

When I opened them again, I had to snap them shut immediately and try several times more. I blinked once, twice, five times to confirm it, but the world had gone and changed on me. Gone was the smell of monsoon air and banana groves. Instead, I sat with my back pressed up to sunlit cobblestones—a crumbling wall, I'd come to realize a few moments later—surrounded by unfamiliar façades, a skyline I did not recognize.

¿Dónde estoy? My first fully articulated thought, and I had no answer to the question. I had no clue where I was. I saw people dressed in fashions vastly different from my own. Looking down at myself, I confirmed that I was still dressed in my uniform. It was still fresh. This led to my second internal question: *¿Qué día es hoy?* I had no guesses about that either. Not but a moment ago, it was nighttime on a Wednesday. Now daylight washed over me, on what day, I did not know.

Wondering and wandering, I found a public plaza in the late afternoon, where some local guards noticed me, a stranger in an unknown uniform. During their interrogation, I learned the truth: I was no longer in Manila at all but in Mexico City, capital of the Viceroyalty of New Spain. I was thousands of kilometers from home, across an entire ocean.

They called me a deserter and charged me with being a "servant of the devil." I shared everything I knew about my governor's death (news they had not yet received), the dizzying haze I fell under, and my awakening in a different land. Day after day, I repeated my story to the Viceroy, to the Inquisition's stoic faces, and to the walls of my cell when no one would listen. I insisted: I'd been guarding the palace in Manila moments before some heretical *magia* spirited me away to Mexico.

It took many long months of waiting in prison until a galleon from the Philippines—a punchline of a ship with terribly delayed timing—arrived in New Spain carrying goods, people, and vital information. Fresh news, specifically the assassination of Governor Gómez Pérez Dasmariñas and the Chinese piracy, confirmed all my claims. Well, that is to say, *almost* everything. Nothing explained how I came to be here in such an inconceivable length of time.

Luck continued to favor me when one of the passengers recognized me. Under oath, he went on record to say he'd seen me in Manila on guard duty at the Palacio del Gobernador the day after they learned of the Governor's death. This was my uncanny vindication. Uncanny and true.

Although my tale defied geography, reason, and religion, the authorities released me and allowed me to return home on the galleon's voyage back to the Philippines.

I've had a hard time falling asleep since my experience. I don't remember the last time I had a good *noche de sueño*. And that's unsurprising, no? Not after learning the hard way that even a moment's rest can deliver you across the world, turn you into a legend.

Rest with care, *mi amigos*.

The Reaper and the Night Nurse

DEATH LIKED THE NIGHT shift best. The halls were quieter, the shadows longer, and the only voices were the murmurs of the dying and the soft drone of the TV in the nurse's lounge. It was in those hours that he first saw her: the night nurse. Her Sacred Heart Hospice employee badge read *E. Harrow*. She moved through the dim corridors of St. Martin's Care Home with a lantern's grace as she checked on residents, adjusted blankets, and hummed old songs to those whose hands now trembled like moth wings. Death, who had seen every variety of endings, found himself lingering. Not because she feared him (few did by the time they arrived here), but *because* of *her*.

Of course, they never spoke; he wasn't built for casual conversation anymore—human words fell from his mouth like ash—but she seemed to sense his presence in the room. He assumed Nurse Harrow was one of those unusual humans with an instinct for finality. She had a habit of arriving moments before he did. He'd enter a room on official business to find her holding a patient's hand and whispering syllables that seemed to soothe their souls. He admired her work. She admired nothing about *his* job, he was sure, but she didn't hate him either.

There came a time when Death sought a man named Charlie Wicks, an eighty-six-year-old former math teacher who now lay in a comfortable, drugged sleep in Room 74 on his last day battling colon cancer. Nurse Harrow was already there, watching Charlie's final breaths rise and fall, a cool washcloth pressed against his forehead. She opened her mouth to speak, but then the dearly departed's spirit finished its detachment from his body. In a sweet and caring gesture, she patted the old man's hand and set about noting the time of death and calling the front desk to summon an orderly.

She had a job to do. So did Death.

They fell into an odd rhythm over the following weeks, an unspoken agreement that their professions were parallel in purpose if not method. He noticed more things: the way she carried extra sweet n' low packets in her pocket for the diabetics who loved their iced tea too sweet; how she adjusted her ponytail before leaning over a patient's bed, so as not to tickle their cheeks; how she wrote her notes in a neat, looping hand, as though it mattered that the living remembered these medical details of the dead.

It was absurd, he knew, to think of her as anything but temporary, since everyone was. Yet absurdity is the cousin of longing, and longing was a rare luxury for him.

The first time Death delayed a reaping inside Sacred Heart Hospice, it was almost by accident. He came for a woman named Pearl early in the night one summer. She had last been awake Easter weekend. An IV drip kept her comfortable, but she was ready to cross over; her heart, which had been beating in a slow cadence, began its final erratic pumps. He glanced toward Nurse Harrow, saw her wrestling with a stubborn blanket in another room, and thought: *I'll wait a minute more.*

Just one minute.

Pearl continued to live until dawn. Long enough for Johnny, her estranged son, to arrive. He was expected yesterday, but a twelve-hour flight delay in St. Louis stalled his arrival. Weeping and sleep-deprived, he made it to her bedside forty-five minutes before she slipped away. *Mercy and Miracles*, the residents and staff at Sacred Heart called it.

And there was no excuse the second time. Harrow fell behind on her rounds, held up by a resident suffering from a sour stomach. She was going to miss the passing of Ricardo Esteban, a longtime equal rights activist and star of the 1978 soap opera *The World Goes On*. Death wanted his favorite nurse to walk into the room, to see her tuck that rogue strand of hair behind her ear as she leaned over this patient one last time. And then, yes, he would do his reaping.

It became a dangerous habit. Procrastinated reapings stacked like books waiting to be read. A year passed in this slow waltz.

The end of it all happened in Room 207.

Harrow sat with Mrs. Coates, a thirty-five-year-old lady finishing her struggle with a quick, brutal cancer. Death came, stood at the ready in his usual position, but the nurse stopped her chorus of comforting reassurances and turned her head to meet Death's gaze, which stunned him dumb.

"I wondered," she said softly, "how long you planned on keeping me."

Those words cracked his porcelain features. "You knew?" he asked.

"Not at first," she replied. Mrs. Coates may have been unaware of her surroundings and the conversations taking place within them, but Harrow went on holding her hand anyway. "My accident in December... the doctors called it a miracle that I survived. But I doubted that very much. Every time you stopped by after that, I could see you. It felt like we already knew each other. But I wasn't sure for a long time that I wasn't just going crazy."

Death said nothing. Words felt useless against the inevitable fate looming between them.

Five months ago, he had received a summons—for *her*. Standing outside her break room at the time, invisible to mortal eyes but feeling oddly like a man about to knock on a lover's door, he watched her sit with a thermos of coffee as she flipped through a paperback murder mystery. A notification chirped on her phone: her Uber ride home was expected to arrive in the next five minutes.

Harrow's hourglass was minutes away from running its course. Death tipped it sideways. *Not today*, he told himself. *And not the next, either*. He cheated, hoarded, and stole days to give to the night nurse—coins pilfered from unattended tills and bank vaults, so he, the Undead Robin Hood, could watch her care for others, to hear her laugh at something another nurse said, to catch the faint scent of her floral hand cream.

But for Death, the ledger does not forgive, and the weight of an undone duty is heavier than most mortals ever understand. His time with Harrow was over. Now he had to make things right.

The night nurse smiled at him. "It was kind of you to give me extra credit."

"It was selfish," he admitted.

"Then we're both guilty of that," she said. She gave Mrs. Coates one final, gentle pat on the hand and got to her feet.

Not for the first time, Death thought that Harrow must be a saint in the modern age, and the way she regarded him now with warm acceptance solidified that notion.

The bittersweet quiet between them lingered over the room, the final pause before closing an excellent book. He offered her his hand; she took it.

"It's time," he said.

She nodded in agreement. "Walk me out?"

And so Death did.

The Nose Knows, Don't Ya Know

When Chris blinked awake one fine Saturday morning, his face felt wrong. The man in the mirror looked wrong, too. The eyes were close enough—still brown and bloodshot—but the rest was someone else's rendering of Christopher Dellweather. The nose, much larger than usual, had a hawkish slope instead of the small upturn he'd had all his life. He felt the chin, squared where it should have pointed. It was like an understudy was called to stand in for his face.

He stumbled from the master bedroom's en suite bathroom. His wife, Cara, didn't flinch at the sight of him. Didn't gasp. Didn't scream "*Who are you and what have you done with my husband?*"

What she actually asked was, "You sleep okay?"

Not knowing what else to do, Chris dragged his hands down his face again. The situation had not changed; the flesh he felt was alien to him. "You...you don't see it?"

She buttoned the jeans she'd just pulled on and regarded him. "See what? You're always a little puffy in the morning, hon."

The kids didn't react either. Fourteen-year-old Evan offered him a high-five on his way out to catch the school bus. Two-year-old Lily played with her cereal at the table. For the fiftieth-some-odd time, Chris traced his jawline with his fingertips on the off chance he might find a zipper that he could open to free his real face. Nothing. There was regular human skin and a two-day stubble—just not *his*.

Without any sort of proper plan of action in place to make sense of this, he went to work. He struggled not to be a distracted driver that day on his way to Mosley Antiquities & Acquisitions. He kept wanting to stare at his features in the rearview mirror. And yet none of his colleagues had anything to say about his new, strange appearance. Not his receptionist. Not his best friend. Not even the retinal scanner he used to enter restricted areas.

About the only good and normal thing about this long, nerve-racking day was when it was finally over and he lay in his warm bed. Cara pressed her head to his chest, murmured something about needing to order mulch before the season rush, but he could only stare at the ceiling fan. He watched it spinning like a roulette wheel until he drifted off to sleep.

He checked his face with his hands upon waking the next morning. He did not like what he felt. What's worse, another new face greeted him in the bathroom mirror. A thinner one this time, pocked with old acne craters and brown freckles.

Same reaction from everyone: none at all.

An idea struck him. He could retrieve his driver's license from his wallet and show the photo on it to Cara and the others. He snatched his pants from the floor and yanked his wallet out of the back pocket. The face on the laminated card *matched*, freckles and all. Chris wanted to laugh. Or scream. Or peel off his skin.

He spoke to a psychiatrist for the first time in his life. They discussed possibilities and arranged to meet twice a week. An appointment was set for him at the neurological center in the next town over for tests and scans.

Chris next awoke with no mouth, a smooth patch of hairless skin in its place. He screamed, but the sound clotted in his throat like wet cotton.

The sound was the only thing Cara noticed. She looked at him over her morning toast and frowned when he staggered into the kitchen. "You know, you always get like this when you're stressed."

Chris shook his head violently. His heart was a runaway jackhammer.

Cara sighed. "Wanna talk about it?"

He jabbed a frantic finger at his face.

She smiled. "But honey, I've always loved that expression on you."

What on Earth could have done this to Chris?

Heisenberg's Uncertain Parent

THEY NAMED THEIR DAUGHTER Nova, after the space storms that swept through Colony Cluster Stations #5-9 in the Delta Calisto Quadrant of the expansive Seratus Galaxy. Her parents landed on this name before her birth, though technically, she *wasn't* born—not in the bio-traditional way. Grown in a quantum embryo suspended in decoherence, she was an engineered human-hybrid.

Quantum incubation was necessary to produce life between Homo-Sapiens and Di-Quarlons. While genders and sexes among Earth-beings were often a complicated matter, the Di-Quarlon did not possess such differentiating factors. Any one of them was capable of impregnating or getting pregnant. Pregnancies between them and other species in the *usual* way failed to come to term, though, and often had devastating effects on the individual who carried the baby. Thus, the development of the Heisenberg Incubation Pod (HIP) was inevitable.

The problem was that none of the Creation models on the market were calibrated for the solar flares plaguing the colony stations. Brought to you by GalaxaPharm's top-of-the-line procreating products, the HIP was the best option for Nova's parents because it boasted triple redundancy, which was really just a pretty word for "three strikes and you're out."

Nova was a betweenworld fetus, developing on schedule when the biggest recorded wave of solar flares struck the colonies. The next moment, Nurse Simone witnessed her collapsing into herself inside a crashing algorithmic cradle incubator, beneath the flicker of emergency backup lights. The solar flares altered her existence. She existed on this plane now because, by pure luck, the morning nurse entered the room at the right moment and saw it happening to her, which stalled the mysterious process partway.

She continued to exist so long as one person had at least one eye on her.

They partially dealt with this unforeseen challenge through jokes.

"She's shy," Jonah would say when friends came to visit. "Our Quantum Girl won't show her face unless someone's watching."

Nova would giggle and babble, hanging onto Di-Jiro-Lan's shoulder as she was carried around. Her body mass shifted like a dream whenever someone looked away from her, a trick of the eye occurring just out of reach of their peripheral vision. Her image often lagged behind her laughter by half a second.

That was probably also the reason video calls glitched. The audio would drop out after a while.

The doctors and scientists said she was *entangled.* A simple, cute word for "stuck in flux." Jonah and Di-Jiro-Lan rewired their entire home with proximity sensors, retinal anchors, and gaze-linked stabilization software. Cameras on swivel mounts, their apartment on Colony #6 became a constant blinking, staring surveillance ecosystem.

Nova's parents loved her like the world was ending—which, in a way, theirs was always on the brink of doing just that.

Parenting got harder when she started to crawl and explore nooks and crannies. Di-Jiro-Lan was the first to suggest the schedule. Six-hour night shifts, taking alternating turns, all breaks timed with bathroom breaks and REM cycles. They took to calling it "quantum parenting," but it was triage really.

They tested the severity of Nova's condition early on. A doctor observed the infant swaddled in a baby blanket, fast asleep. The second doctor turned his back on them. A blink. A coffee sip. A moment or two more would lapse. On cue, the second doctor cleared his throat. In response, the first doctor closed his eyes.

The sound was not loud; it was more like a small sigh. The blanket collapsed in and filled up again, as the baby shifted in and out of reality. No crying. No flashy show. Just *almost* gone and back again, more gone than back with each passing moment. Both doctors then turned to look at Nova, and she was there again, *all the way* there. Lying exactly where she had been, as though nothing weird had just happened.

What needed to be done was crystal clear: someone must be observing Nova for her to exist.

Most people who knew them expected it would be Di-Jiro-Lan who blinked too long. He was the one who fell asleep during movies, who dozed easily on planes, trains, and space shuttles. But it was Jonah.

Nova didn't like bedtime. Not because of monsters or the fear of disappearing, but because toddlers are natural chaos demons when it comes to matters like going to bed. Jonah sat in the rocking chair, one foot gently tapping the floor, with Nova curled against his chest like a question mark wrapped in a blanket. He read aloud from a picture book she liked. Nova's soft babble—something about cats—was beginning to have a hypnotic effect on him.

"Shhh," Jonah whispered. "Close your eyes."

Reassured by the kiss to her forehead, she smiled in return and yawned, her lashes already fluttering closed. So were his.

A blink.

A second blink.

A third longer blink.

It was the creak of the chair that woke him. Or maybe it was the silence. A later review of the surveillance showed he had fallen asleep for two minutes and nine seconds. His arms were empty. The room was the same as it was before—except no Nova. Jonah bolted to his feet, caught in the molasses of mounting parental fear.

He called her name. Called it again. And again, even louder.

Dashing around in a panic, he checked the crib, the bathroom, the hallway, and the cabinets. He shouted her name in every room and checked every hidden corner, turned on all the lights and sensors. He tripped the whole house into emergency mode, but all to no avail.

Nova had vanished.

The psychiatry team in charge of their grief counseling later would be able to review the exact nanosecond, through system files and footage, that she left this plane. But the real grief was that there was no equation for her retrieval.

Di-Jiro-Lan returned home from book club an hour later and found Jonah's tall, lanky body crammed into Nova's bed, whispering her name like a prayer.

"I didn't mean to," he cried. "I just blinked. It felt like a *blink.*"

Surveillant helper-bots whirred like wasps overhead. Ordinarily, they were used to monitor children (though they did not prevent Nova from fluctuating, they were useful for other aspects of parenting); they also scanned and interpreted adults. When these bots registered Di-Jiro-Lan and Jonah's behavior and vital signs, several alerts were flagged in their protocols. After observing three days of worsening mental condition and no contact with the outside world, they sent out an Emergency Medical and Wellness Concern to the proper authorities, which prompted the physical check-in by health agents that led to the start of Di-Jiro-Lan and Jonah's treatment plan for grieving.

Drones delivered groceries. Therapists visited four times a week for the first month and once a week for the next six. Activities were logged, taxes processed. And all the worlds in the universe kept turning.

It was quite the shock to everyone when Nova reappeared twenty-six years later as a fifteen-year-old girl, stepping confidently into the kitchen from a sudden time rift that disrupted her parents' dinner party.

Dark & Bright

Clouds as dark as tree bark,
And still the sun forces through
Slim rays for these fateful days —
The time I get to spend with you.

Old Haskin's Shop of Oddities

WELL, HELLO THERE, STRANGER! You must be new in town. I know just about every local face here, and I've never seen yours. Are you on vacation or movin' here? Ah, never mind. Old women like me tend to be nosy. I don't mean nothin' by it. If you're doin' some shoppin' or maybe a little sightseein', make sure you check out Old Haskin's Shop of Oddities over yonder. Don't know how he stays afloat with the strange things he sells!

What do I mean? Well, last Thursday, he sold a cuckoo clock that—no kiddin'—is always twenty-four hours ahead. Not fast. *Ahead.* The dang mechanized bird pops out at the top of the hour and screams about what's gonna happen tomorrow. The first couple to buy it—oh, this would have been three or four years ago now—brought it back three days later, pale as flour, and would say not a word about what that clock told them.

Oh, that's nothin'! You should see the Victorian armchair in the corner, the deep burgundy one with the high back that probably saw more drama than a soap opera. Everyone who sits on it immediately jumps up, mutterin' somethin' different. My cousin yelled, "Get out before the fire starts!" Then right after, his girlfriend said, "It's under the floorboards." Ain't nobody knows what any of it means, but Old Haskin seems amused by the effect. Keeps it tagged at $19,740."

Don't believe me? Whatcha gonna think when I tell you I was browsin' in there just last week when this dusty teapot started whistlin' its head off. And not because it was heatin' on a stovetop—heck, *there was no stove*. It resides in a crowded china cabinet! Old Haskin says it's been doin' that on and off for years. I think it's tryin' to send a message: "*Stop comin' here if you're not gonna buy nothin'*."

Speakin' of kitchen paraphernalia, y'know how folks like to tap a glass with a spoon to announce they're about to give a speech? Well, in that shop, if you do that with the silver spoons in the display case, they hit back. I heard about this one kid who was playin' around in there, using a pair of them silver spoons like drumsticks. He got to drummin' out beats on the merchandise, and Old Haskin told him to stop unless he wanted those spoons to knock a tooth out. His parents were *not* happy about that dental bill. Ask anyone in town!

Come, cross the street with me and see for yourself. I'll show you around.

Take a minute to admire the items in the storefront window before we go inside. Yes, that *is* an ancient Remington typewriter on sale. Been on display for a while. People pass by, admirin' it through the glass, but never buy. All the keys are either jammed or broken off, 'cept the letters to spell "SORRY." Plus, it has a mind of its own. Every mornin', Old Haskin finds a fresh sheet in it with that word typed over and over. I've seen him pullin' it out of its mouth on more than one occasion, on my way to early appointments. Seems to me, the margins get a little tighter each time.

Ready to head in and look around? Lemme get the door for you. Yeah, yeah, I know what you're thinkin'. Smells like mothballs and mystery in here, don't it? If I'm not mistaken, the oldest thing for sale is the creepy doll on that middle shelf. Sometimes it's holdin' a little parasol in its left hand. Sometimes in the right. Haskin swears he's never touched it himself, and I believe him, on account of the times I've caught it winkin' at me. Hand to God, it's the truth.

Be right back. I'll let the proprietor know he has a visitor. Why don't you check out my favorite item: that seven-foot-tall antique gilt mirror? No matter who stands in front of it, someone else is always reflected back at them. If you try to take a selfie, the pictures show an empty mirror with no one in it, not even the photographer.

I'm back! Old Haskins welcomes you. He'll be right out—important business call and all that, you understand.

Ah, you're admirin' the sweet little wind-up ballerina box. Open it, and instead of music, you'll hear a crackle like one of those vintage ham radios. It forecasts the weather in Russia.

Nobody listens for long. Endless bad weather warnin's are a total mood killer.

Oh, yes, that's right. There is a whole other room to browse beyond the partially open parlor door ahead of you.

Wait! Before you go that way, come and see the stacks of receipts and ledgers on the counter behind the register. Perfectly normal for an oddities shop that's been there since forever, but the one on the very tippy-top? That first page is always blank when you first look at it. Only for a second, 'cuz—see there! It's already changin' right before your very own peepers. The looker's name appears in ink with the words "Transaction Pending" underneath it. Spectacular magic, am I right?

Well, I'll leave you to it then! Oh, and don't skip the discount book bin. I've got a feelin' there's somethin' in there you won't wanna put down. Stories have a way of findin' the right reader, and you seem like the type who leaves a lastin' impression.

Happy shoppin', my friend!

Acknowledgments

Kristi Eskew wears many hats—writer, executive editor, boss, mentor, mother, friend, and so many others—and she wears them all with uncommon grace. As my editor, she asked the right questions, caught what I missed, and knew exactly when to push and when to trust the work. As my boss at Bookstr, she has been a steady champion of writers and stories, leading with incredible professionalism, patience, generosity, and a deep respect for craft. This book is sharper, stranger, and more itself because of her care and insight. If you're an independent writer looking for an editor, you are making the right choice when you enlist her services. Keep an eye out for her newest venture, Pointed Prose, featuring the writing community, For the Plot.

You can find Kristi and learn more about her editorial services on Instagram @kristi_eskew87 and https://kmeskew.wordpress.com/.

And tell her my book sent you.

ABOUT THE AUTHOR

Erin Dzielski believes science and fantasy get along just fine—heck, they often throw better parties together. In addition to independently publishing her novels, she writes and edits for Bookstr, where she covers books, culture, and the strange magic that happens when stories meet audiences. She is a wife and mother living in North Carolina with her husband, children, dogs, bunnies, budgies, and chickens. When she's not working, Erin can usually be found reading, researching something delightfully obscure, playing video games, or dreaming up stories that blur the lines between the real and the impossible.

You can keep up with her on LinkedIn or Instagram (@erindzielski) for bookish entertainment and previews of upcoming releases. You can also read her Bookstr articles, blogs, and interviews at https://bookstr.com/author/erin-dzielski/.

www.ingramcontent.com/pod-product-compliance
Lightning Source LLC
LaVergne TN
LVHW090602110826
845146LV00001B/236

* 9 7 9 8 9 9 5 0 9 4 0 8 1 *